"Lush and picaresque… a master novelist not to be missed"

Oprah.com

"The richness of Kurniawan's storytelling will leave you chuckling and amazed, begging for more" *CounterPunch*

"Scatological, scandalous, lively, beautiful and dark and messed up and fantastical. It's like *One Hundred Years of Solitude* kicked into another gear, with almost a punk sensibility housed within gorgeous writing – and stories coiled within stories within stories"

Jeff Van der Meer, author of the *Southern Reach* trilogy

"The final wonder of *Beauty Is a Wound* is how much pure liveliness and joy there is mixed up with the pain" *Saturday Paper*

PUSHKIN PRESS

VENGEANCE IS MINE, ALL OTHERS PAY CASH

EKA KURNIAWAN was born in Tasikmalaya, Indonesia in 1975. He studied philosophy at Gadjah Mada University, Yogyakarta and has since published several novels and short stories. He was longlisted for the Man Booker International Prize 2016 and his books have been translated into 33 languages. His highly acclaimed, epic work of magical realism *Beauty is a Wound* is also available from Pushkin Press.

"A tragicomedy Indonesian thriller… By turns a soft porn flick, a manic road thriller and a martial arts movie… A blast of a book"
Financial Times

"Hard-boiled pulp fiction… written with literary flair, commenting on Indonesia's history and sense of nationhood while delivering gangster thrills"
Herald

"A potent blend of grounded realism and flighty fantasy… a pulpy, visceral tale of sex, violence and comeuppance" *Economist*

"Thrilling… engrossing, emotionally rankling speed-read… original and sure-footed" *Big Issue*

"An almost unbelievably fun and weird novel"
Publishers Weekly (starred review)

"Like a Tarantino movie: as a sort of bravura, X-rated pantomime, delivered with style and panache… superb" *Asian Review of Books*

"Keeps th̲e̲ ̲t̲e̲n̲s̲i̲o̲n̲ ̲p̲o̲i̲n̲t̲ the reader on… An excellent r̲e̲a̲d̲,̲ List (blog)

700043985320

Praise for
BEAUTY IS A WOUND

"An old-school gothic folk tale, full of dark magic, hyperbole and gratuitous violence"　　　　　　　　　　　　　　　　　　*Guardian*, Books of the Year

"A howling masterpiece"　　　　　　　　　　　　　　　Chigozie Obioma,
author of the Man Booker-shortlisted *The Fishermen*

"A literary child of Günter Grass, Gabriel García Márquez and Salman Rushdie"　　　　　　　　　　　　　　　　　*New York Review of Books*

"The best book I read last year… A blistering critique of Indonesia's bloody past, lightly and variously veiled as a horror story, a farce, a romance, and a B-movie sex romp – but shot through, too, with a strangely touching, light-hearted compassion"　　　　　　　　　　　　　　*New Yorker*

"A glorious melange of comic grotesquery, romance and political satire"
Asian Review of Books

"Without a doubt the most original, imaginatively profound, and elegant writer of fiction in Indonesia today"　　　　　　　*New Left Review*

"Kurniawan does not merely traffic skillfully in magic realism; his Halimunda – like García Márquez's Macondo and Faulkner's Yoknapatawpha County – lets him show how the currents of history catch, whirl, carry away and sometimes drown people"　　　　　　　　　　*New York Times*

"Original and powerful… Maybe, who knows, the judges of the Nobel Prize could, in a few years, consider giving [Eka] the prize that Indonesia has never received"　　　　　　　　　　　　　　　　　　*Le Monde*

"An epic picaresque that's equal parts *Canterbury Tales* and *Mahabharata* – exuberantly excessive and captivating"　　　　　　　*Kirkus Review*

"Upon finishing the book, the reader will have the sense of encountering not just the history of Indonesia but its soul and spirit… An astounding, momentous book"　　　　　　　　　　　　　　　　*Publishers Weekly*

Eka Kurniawan

Vengeance Is Mine, All Others Pay Cash

TRANSLATED BY ANNIE TUCKER

PUSHKIN PRESS

Pushkin Press
71–75 Shelton Street,
London WC2H 9JQ

Seperti Dendam, Rindu Harus Dibayar Tuntas © Eka Kurniawan, 2014
By Agreement with Pontas Literary & Film Agency.
Translation © 2017 by Annie Tucker

First published in 2014 by PT Gramedia Pustaka Utama, Jakarta
Published in English in the United States by New Directions in 2017
First published by Pushkin Press in 2017
This edition first published in 2018

1 3 5 7 9 8 6 4 2

ISBN 13: 978-1-78227-428-5

Offset by Tetragon, London
Printed in Great Britain by the CPI Group, UK

www.pushkinpress.com

For Ratih Kumala

❊1❊

"ONLY GUYS WHO can't get hard fight with no fear of death," Iwan Angsa once said about Ajo Kawir. He was one of a small handful of people who knew that Ajo Kawir's penis couldn't stand up. He'd seen it, nestling like a newly hatched baby bird—curled into itself, looking hungry and cold. Sometimes in the morning when its owner had just awoken, it seemed longer, full of urine, but it couldn't stand up. It couldn't get hard.

—

Ajo Kawir sat on the edge of his bed, naked. He was looking down at his crotch, gazing at his pecker which seemed to be resting in an eternal slumber, so lazy. He whispered to it, get up, Bird. Get up, you Wretch. You can't just sleep forever. You have to get up. But that damn little bird didn't want to get up.

He thought about that girl. Iteung.

You have to get up, he whispered again, for her. That girl wants you. She wants you to wake up and get big and hard, the way you used to. You loser, get up. I'm out of patience. I want you to get up. Now.

But the Bird thought it was a polar bear hibernating through a long frigid winter. It was dreaming of gently falling snow, which its master had never even seen.

He went into the bathroom. He stuck a page ripped out of an old crossword puzzle magazine up on the wall. It was a photograph of a singer. He didn't know her name but he liked her face, and her body even more. She was wearing nothing but a low-cut bikini. Her breasts swelled as if they were trying to pop free of her body, but what he liked best of all was her armpit hair, thick and black. He imagined what those armpits must smell like.

Ajo Kawir splashed water all over his body and he calmed down a little. Scooping up more water from the tub, he poured it over his head and a feeling of refreshment settled over him. His hair stuck to his forehead and his ears. Water dripped off the tip of his nose and his chin.

I'm going to try again, he thought. He looked at the photograph. Eyeing the woman's cleavage and her thick black armpit hair, he took hold of his penis. Stroked it.

Get up, he whispered.

He picked up the bar of soap and rubbed it in between his hands. He closed his eyes for a moment, and then grasped his penis again.

Get up, he whispered. Wake up, you clown, he whimpered, softly like a dog in heat.

But this Bird thought it was a polar bear and now was the time to hibernate. This Bird was sleeping soundly. Dreaming of snow.

Shit, Ajo Kawir grumbled.

———

Gecko also knew that Ajo Kawir's penis refused to wake up. That's why Gecko never invited him along to loiter in front of the post office and catcall the girls passing by, and why he never invited him to watch pornos together and never loaned him any trashy novels, believing that things like that wouldn't cure the kid, but in fact would only aggravate him. And guys who can't get hard should never be aggravated—after everything that happened, that's what Iwan Angsa would admonish him.

—

They were walking along the sidewalk, each with a clove cigarette between his fingers. One was sucking on a Djarum, the other had never strayed from Gudang Garams. Gecko placed the clove in his mouth, let it hang there, and slipped both his hands into the pockets of his jeans. He bit the cigarette a little so it wouldn't fall when he exhaled. The smoke slowly emerged from his mouth, and with the finesse of a longtime smoker he inhaled the plume back up through his nose and then exhaled it out his mouth again, in a smooth rolling circle.

Ajo Kawir gazed up at the sky and blew his own fragrant smoke into the air. Then, looking over at Gecko, he said, "I want to beat someone up."

"How about those two kids sitting against that wall over there."

Ajo Kawir glanced to where Gecko was pointing and saw two guys who looked to be about their age, whistling at the girls passing by on their bicycles. Ajo Kawir and Gecko approached. Ajo Kawir took a long final drag on his cigarette. There were still about three centimeters left until it was down to the butt, but Ajo Kawir knew he didn't want anymore—instead he tossed it, with its red-hot tip, into one of the guy's laps. They both looked up at Ajo Kawir, startled.

"Hey!" they shouted, angry of course.

"You got a problem?" challenged Ajo Kawir.

Gecko opened and closed his fists, to limber up his fingers. It was going to be an awesome afternoon, he thought. It was going to be exciting, a fun fight.

—

Ajo Kawir was good at finding trouble—he didn't care if it meant the night would leave him black and blue. Sometimes his scuffles wound up with him in the village trustee's house, sometimes at the police station, and sometimes lying facedown unconscious in an irrigation ditch. One had even ended in the emergency room. And what could Gecko do, he'd never let his friend get beaten to a pulp all alone without any backup, so he frequently ended up covered with bruises too.

Wa Sami, who despaired at their behavior, could only twist their ears and yell at them, "Ya Allah, could you guys stop acting like such useless creatures, once and for all?"

"God says that nothing in this world is useless," said Gecko.

"Don't be such a know-it-all. You don't have the slightest idea what God says."

—

In this whole business, Gecko felt terribly guilty, even though Ajo Kawir never blamed him. Gecko would have done whatever it took to atone for his mistake, but he knew that there was nothing in the world he could do to fix all the problems he had caused.

"If I could give you mine," he said once, "I would do it in a heartbeat."

"I don't need your fucking bird."

"I know you don't need it, but I guarantee you, my dick is really good."

"Shut up! I don't want to hear you whine on and on about your wrongdoings. You didn't do anything wrong. If it was anyone's fault, it was mine. I was wrong and now I'm paying the price. But I'm the one who has the right to complain, not you. Just go live your life. Sleep with as many women as you can—think of me while you do them, if you want, but I'm telling you, don't waste what you have. As long as your pecker works, take girls to bed. They need it. There is not one woman alive who doesn't want to get laid."

Gecko let it drop. He didn't want to make Ajo Kawir any more depressed. He didn't want to remind Ajo Kawir of his terrible fate. Instead, he'd invite his friend out, to help him forget his troubles. He would fight by his side, if that would release all the pent-up adolescent desire that couldn't be released through his privates.

Or he'd buy his friend a bottle of Bintang beer.

—

It all started years ago, long before Ajo Kawir went to Jakarta and became a truck driver and met a woman named Jelita. It happened when the boys were still only twelve or thirteen years old, or about that age. Those kinds of details grow fuzzy with time, but every single thing happened to them that night was still crystal clear in their memory.

—

They left the *surau* where—mostly as a way to get out of the house—they studied prayer recitation. They lived on the outskirts of the city, and the *surau* was by the side of the road. They walked down the narrow alleyways cutting in between the houses and then turned. For days now they'd turned at that same corner, always heading for the village headman's house.

They hid in the shadows. They crept toward the window and

peeked inside. The headman had just gotten married for the third time, and now he was in bed with his newest wife. The newlyweds had barely been married a week and were still full of enthusiastic lust.

"I like her boobs," Ajo Kawir whispered to Gecko. "Like a pair of young coconuts."

"More like papayas."

"Look, Mister Headman is putting his thing in between his wife's breasts."

"Yeah, I want to try that one day when I'm married."

"Just pray that your wife has boobs that big."

"Of course they'll be that big."

Ajo Kawir groped at his pants, readjusting his dick, which had gotten bigger and was no longer comfortable. He kept on holding it, as if he never wanted to let go.

"Did you come?"

"Mmm."

They returned to the *surau*. Ajo Kawir went to the small bathroom around the back and cleaned himself up, while Gecko lay down on the terrace, on a roomy couch next to the big *beduk* drum that was beaten to call people to prayer. Gecko daydreamed about the shape of the headman's wife's breasts and wondered who out of all of his classmates would end up having boobs that big. He recited all their names in his head and thought that one day he'd propose to one of them. On their wedding night, he vowed he would place his member in her cleavage.

Ajo Kawir finished washing up and emerged trying to dry his wet hair by rubbing the strands between the palms of his hands.

"Why did you bathe this late at night?"

"I came."

"So what? I came too."

"I want to do the *tahajjud* prayer."

"For God's sake, why?"

"Who knows, maybe my sins can be erased."

"What happened back there wasn't a sin."

"Yes it was."

Gecko didn't like to argue. He let Ajo Kawir go into the *surau*. He wasn't sure whether the *tahajjud* prayer could be used for something like that or not, and he didn't care. The boys could recite the Koran, but they hadn't really learned anything. All he knew was that they were supposed to pray five times a day, but they hardly ever did.

—

Ajo Kawir went to Wa Sami's corner store, sat in a chair, and took out some comic books. Wa Sami asked, what comics are those? Kids these days read too many comics, and that's why they're so foolish and dim-witted. Ajo Kawir showed her his comics. But these are comics about heaven and hell, he said. Even the kyai at the *surau* thinks these comics are great. Well that's good then, that you're reading those comics, said Wa Sami. I didn't know there were comics like that.

"Here it shows that if we kill a mosquito, in hell a giant mosquito will kill *us*. It will kill us over and over again, and we will die over and over again."

"You must never kill," said Wa Sami.

"And if we steal, a cleaver will chop off our hand. It'll be chopped off, and then it will grow back, get chopped off, grow back, chopped off, like that forever."

"You must never steal."

"Iwan Angsa murdered and stole."

"He has repented."

"So, if I murder and steal, then I can also repent."

"Apparently those comics haven't been too useful for that brain of yours."

———

That night, Gecko discovered something even more interesting than the breasts of the headman's wife and the newlywed's love-making, and he wanted to share his secret with Ajo Kawir.

"*Astagfirullah!*" exclaimed Ajo Kawir. "Can't we find another game?! I don't want to go to hell and have my dick bitten off by a pussy with teeth."

Gecko had never heard of a pussy with teeth, and he didn't want to think about one right now. He cajoled his friend, saying that if he went alone then it wouldn't be as exciting, that if they repented afterward, their sins would be forgiven (he had heard that from their kyai at the *surau*).

Well, if it's really even more interesting, said Ajo Kawir reluctantly, then let's go see.

———

Neither Iwan Angsa nor Wa Sami realized that something extraordinary was going to happen to Ajo Kawir and Gecko that night. They rarely took much notice when Gecko went out after dark.

Ajo Kawir arrived ten minutes before the agreed upon time, and Gecko walked Iwan Angsa's bike out from the kitchen. He told Ajo Kawir to sit on the back, and they left without telling anyone.

During the journey, Ajo Kawir asked repeatedly where they were going and who they were going to see. Gecko only replied, "Shut your mouth and you'll soon find out!"

———

And ever since that night, Gecko felt incredibly guilty for getting Ajo Kawir mixed up in bad things. Fundamentally Ajo Kawir was a good kid, that's what Gecko would say. Out of all their playmates, Ajo Kawir was the most diligent about going to the *surau*. In school, his grades were never shameful—or at least, not as shameful as Gecko's were. And in his free time, he could usually be found chasing after the roving librarian who came around three times a day on his bicycle. Ajo Kawir read all kinds of books, but who knows why, he talked most about the comics depicting the tortures of hell. Gecko guessed that his friend had found out about the pussies with teeth that bit the dicks off adulterous men from those comics. Maybe it was because of those pictures that he was so afraid of going to hell.

Remembering all of that, Gecko would often think that it would have been better if he'd never brought Ajo Kawir to his secret place that night.

—

But he did. That night they followed the deserted main road. Only one or two vehicles passed by. The city buses had already stopped running. After leaving their neighborhood, the street cut through rice fields that stretched out on either side, passing under the mahogany trees that lined the roadside, and heading for the center of town.

"Where are we going?"

"You'll see."

Gecko brought Ajo Kawir to a house. It wasn't far from the road, but it was a bit secluded, with the closest neighbors about a hundred or two hundred yards away. When Ajo Kawir realized whose house it was he grew uneasy, even a little bit afraid—that was Scarlet Blush's house. Ajo Kawir quickly said that Wa Sami had told them many times not to bother that woman, and he didn't want to, he didn't even want to catch sight of her.

But Gecko replied, "Just shut up and wait! You've never seen anything like this."

—

The kids knew Scarlet Blush was a madwoman who often went berserk. None of them had actually ever seen one of her fits, but she was clearly crazy. She always stayed inside her house alone, refusing to talk to anyone but sometimes laughing to herself, or shrieking for no reason. It was said that people once came from the social welfare office and tried to take her away, but she went nuts and bit one of them—no one could be sure whether that had actually happened, but no one ever tried to move her from her house again.

—

Take this to Scarlet Blush's house, Wa Sami would say to Gecko, holding out a sack filled with rice, instant noodles, a few hunks of salted fish, potatoes, long beans, and who knows what else. Wa Sami would remind him—leave it in front of her door. You don't need to knock and you don't need to talk to her. Scarlet Blush doesn't want to talk to anyone.

Gecko would take his bicycle and strap the sack to the back.

"Don't talk to her."

"I won't. Who wants to talk to a crazy woman?"

He'd go to the house and place the sack by the front door. He had no desire to talk to its inhabitant and didn't stay there very long. The neighborhood kids said that the woman's husband still lived there, as a ghost. Gecko wasn't afraid of ghosts—he'd never actually seen a ghost, but why would he talk to a madwoman or hang around her house? He always just put the sack in front of the door and left right away.

"She'll take that food, and she'll live on it," said Wa Sami.

"But why do you care about that crazy woman?"

"Because she used to be my friend. She's still my friend, actually, but she doesn't want to talk to anyone anymore."

—

But one day Gecko decided not to go home right away. He lingered for a few minutes, standing outside Scarlet Blush's front door, wondering, what did a crazy woman do all alone in her house? Do crazy women know how to cook? Curious, he walked around the side of the house and discovered something so interesting that he forgot all about Wa Sami's prohibition.

—

The daughter of a tofu factory owner, Scarlet Blush had eloped with a thief named Agus Cornpipe (or at least, that's what everybody called him). After some time spent as fugitives from the law, going from place to place, they moved into that house. Some said the police were after Agus Cornpipe because during one of his burglaries he'd killed a security guard, and the guy turned out to be an off-duty cop. Others said the police had been hired by his rich father-in-law, who was pissed that Agus Cornpipe had run off with his daughter, it was as simple as that. But in the end, the couple lived in that house and after they befriended a local soldier, the police no longer dared to bother them.

Iwan Angsa had been good friends with Agus Cornpipe, and it was actually Iwan Angsa who had found them the house. Scarlet Blush and Agus Cornpipe had believed they could finally settle down, that no one was hunting them anymore. But they were wrong.

A squadron (years later they realized that it was a troop of soldiers) came to that house. An article in the paper reported that Agus Cornpipe had been armed and had fought back before they shot him dead.

But some people said the soldiers stormed the house, shooting blindly, and that Agus Cornpipe was riddled with bullets, right in front of Scarlet Blush as they were eating dinner. His blood splashed across his wife's face—and it wasn't just blood that sprayed out of the bullet holes, so did his stomach worms and the rice he'd just eaten. Others said the shooting occurred when the couple was in their bedroom making love. The soldiers made Agus Cornpipe finish his last orgasm in heaven. But the version that made the most sense had just one sniper carrying out the execution, shooting from a hiding place behind some trees when Agus Cornpipe opened the window.

In any case, in all versions of the story, Agus Cornpipe was shot to death right before his wife's eyes.

—

"How did Agus Cornpipe really die? Which story is true?"

"I don't know," said Iwan Angsa. "I wasn't there, and no one was there for sure except for Scarlet Blush and the men who did the deed. Whoever shot him will never tell, and as we know, Scarlet Blush will never talk about what happened either."

"But what did he do, exactly? Why did they have to kill him?"

"People don't like thieves roaming around, and the police didn't want to have to deal with it. His family didn't want anything to do with him, and his father-in-law *really* didn't care what happened."

"Who was his family?"

"That's enough," said Wa Sami. "I don't want to talk about this anymore."

—

For weeks, no one wanted to approach that house. No one wanted to take care of Agus Cornpipe's body. Scarlet Blush sat in front of her husband's corpse, hugging her knees and weeping continuously, her clothes splattered with his blood. But then, after a while, she started babbling and grinning to herself. No one knows how she survived in front of that slowly rotting corpse—the only reason no one else was bothered by the smell was because the house was so far away from her nearest neighbors.

Finally, some policemen came. They took photographs and they dragged Agus Cornpipe out back behind the house, wrapped him in a burial shroud, and dug a pit. They forced Scarlet Blush to keep that corpse in her own backyard. Without a gravestone.

—

Gecko circled around the house that day, peering inside. The interior was messy and full of garbage, the chairs and tables were overturned, clothes were hanging everywhere. He had never seen the inside of the house before, so he didn't know whether it had ever been clean. Iwan Angsa had told him that Wa Sami went there every once in a while to tidy up the place, but not to talk. Everyone knew that the madwoman didn't want to talk.

But it turned out that Scarlet Blush actually *did* talk. Gecko realized this because when he saw her he also heard her—Scarlet Blush was talking to herself. She was sitting on a small bench staring at the empty floor before her. Maybe that was the spot where Agus Cornpipe's corpse had lain covered in blood. Her voice was barely audible and he didn't know what she was saying exactly, but she was speaking.

———

If she was more or less in her right mind—or at least this is what Gecko was thinking—Scarlet Blush would open the front door and take the rice and whatever else he had put there for her. She would go to the kitchen and cook, while humming songs from the seventies. After that she would eat on her little bench, staring at the bare floor. Sometimes a kitten would come in and she would let it eat off her plate. And the pieces of leftover food would spill around her, and would still be scattered there days later, rotting and covered with ants.

One day Gecko saw Scarlet Blush, sitting in the middle of what was left of her food, among the cockroaches, playing with the carcass of some random lizard and talking to herself. But all of a sudden she stood up and starting pacing back and forth slowly. She stood in front of a large mirror, looking at her reflection, smiling.

Scarlet Blush swatted at the rotten crumbs stuck to her clothes, but they weren't easy to get off. Then Gecko saw something that he never could have predicted—Scarlet Blush began to take off her clothes.

"Oh lord," he whispered.

Underneath her untidy appearance, the woman still had the body of a teenager. Even the silently spying thirteen-year-old kid realized how attractive she was. Gecko trembled and held on tight to the windowsill.

The woman finished taking off her clothes and walked toward the bathroom. Gecko had to stand on his tiptoes to see her kneel on the bathroom floor, under the water pouring down from the faucet. Her hair was wet, her face was wet, her body was wet.

The kid shook harder, and now there also seemed to be something wet inside his shorts. He groped inside his briefs, holding his privates. They were warm. He enjoyed doing this while watching the village headman make love, and now he enjoyed doing it while watching Scarlet Blush naked under the faucet. He swore that Scarlet Blush was more interesting than anything he'd seen of the village headman's wife.

—

"You're hiding something," Ajo Kawir accused Gecko. "I know you're hiding something. You've never hidden anything from me before, but now you're hiding something."

"You'll find out soon enough," Gecko said.

"What is it?"

"Later you'll know. I won't hide it from you. It's just the opposite, I'll enjoy it more if I can share it with you."

"Did you find a wild chicken laying eggs?"

"It's nothing like that."

Ajo Kawir didn't like that Gecko was keeping a secret from him. They were best friends. They'd trusted each other ever since they were babies. But maybe there were one or two things that they couldn't share; they were slowly growing up. Ajo Kawir would have to understand that, and he tried to understand. They didn't have to discuss every little thing.

"You're in love."

"It's nothing like that. This is something we can enjoy together, but not right now. I'll show you soon."

"Okay, whatever you say."

—

A few days later, hoping to encounter the same sight again, Gecko had snuck off to Scarlet Blush's house in secret. Clearly it wouldn't happen all the time, not even if he waited by the window all day without taking a break.

Of course he wanted to tell Ajo Kawir about this incredible discovery. But how could he invite Ajo Kawir along if he didn't know what day or what time the woman would take off her clothes to bathe? Without that amazing view, there was nothing interesting to share with Ajo Kawir, and so for a while he kept it to himself and didn't say a word to his friend.

—

Gecko finally saw Scarlet Blush go into the bathroom again. He'd made a hole in the wall near the kitchen windowsill, to have a better view if and when it happened. But the woman went into the bathroom just to take a crap, and her shit fell onto the bathroom floor. Cursing, Gecko left.

Then one night, when he was riding his bicycle alone past that house, it occurred to him that he'd go see what Scarlet Blush might be up to at a late hour, and he slunk toward the window. A dim light glowed inside, and from where he stood he saw something else that he knew he had to tell Ajo Kawir about.

But Gecko was in no hurry and a few nights after that, furtive and alone, he went back and saw the same thing again. Now he had figured out the schedule.

He couldn't hold himself back any longer and had to invite Ajo Kawir, saying, "This is way more awesome than anything we've seen at the village headman's house. It's true that her boobs aren't as big, but believe me, this is way more amazing."

—

And now there they were, a few minutes before the stroke of midnight.

As usual, Gecko leaned his bicycle against a mahogany tree far from the house and crept stealthily toward the window. Ajo Kawir followed him from behind. Gecko had already prepared two holes for them to spy through, and directed Ajo Kawir to stand to the left of the window. He peeked into the house while gesturing to Ajo Kawir to do the same.

Inside, Scarlet Blush was sitting on her small bench like usual. Her clothes were stained with some unrecognizable sauce.

Ajo Kawir looked at Gecko, confused. "What's she doing?"

"Just wait," Gecko whispered, reminding Ajo Kawir to keep his voice down.

Ajo Kawir didn't understand what they were waiting for. The woman was exactly as he'd expected: there was nothing to see but a crazy lady playing with her leftover dinner.

That night Scarlet Blush didn't sing any songs from the seventies, and she didn't talk to herself either. She drew her knees up, resting her chin on them, one hand hugging her shins and the other pawing at the rice on her plate. Ajo Kawir looked back at Gecko, asking for some explanation. But Gecko stayed quiet, waiting patiently for what he was certain would soon come to pass.

Almost fifteen minutes went by with Ajo Kawir fending off droning mosquitos. Fed up, he indicated that he was leaving and headed off toward their stashed bicycle. Gecko hurried after him, gesturing for his friend to crouch down.

"Listen," whispered Gecko.

Ajo Kawir strained to hear something.

A motorcycle with its headlight turned off slowly approached and stopped at the front yard of the house. A moment later the engine was cut. There were two men on the motorcycle, looking like ghostly silhouettes. They both dismounted and walked slowly toward the front door.

"It would be better if she wasn't crazy," one of them said.

"But if she wasn't crazy, we wouldn't be here. Be grateful for what's in front of you. My old religion teacher always used to tell us that."

"Whatever. I still wish she wasn't crazy."

Ajo Kawir tried to figure out who had come. He peered into the front room of the house, but the view was obstructed and the two men hadn't even gone inside yet. He pushed himself away from his peephole and moved back a bit, hoping that he could see the two newcomers in the yard in front of the house. But it seemed as though they were already hidden behind the wall, near the door.

"Who are they?" Ajo Kawir whispered.

"Just wait, and don't move around so much, dummy."

Not long after, they could hear someone trying to open the door. Gecko and Ajo Kawir eagerly squinted through their peepholes. The woman was still sitting in the same position as before, as if she didn't hear the sound of a doorknob turning and a door opening.

"They must have a key."

"I know."

Now Ajo Kawir and Gecko could tell who had come. Two policemen. At least, that was what they looked like from their uniforms—the boys didn't recognize them. In the dim light, all they could see was that one of them had a scar cutting across his chin, almost splitting his lip.

Scarface approached Scarlet Blush and kicked her backside, barking, "Go take a bath!" Scarlet Blush didn't move and Scarface kicked her again, and again ordered, "Go take a bath!"

The other cop sat on a chair in a corner, took out a clove cigarette, lit it and began to smoke. He raised one of his legs, resting the sole of his boot on the wall, leaned his head back, and continued to smoke, staring up at the ceiling.

"This crazy woman smells terrible."

"I don't think she's bathed for three days."

Scarface kicked her once again. Scarlet Blush still didn't budge. Impatient, Scarface finally just grabbed the collar of her dress, pulling the woman up. He dragged Scarlet Blush staggering to the bathroom, and shoved her inside. She almost slammed into the wall, but fell right underneath the faucet. Scarface turned on the water and it cascaded down over Scarlet Blush's body.

—

Outside, a light drizzle was falling. The air grew colder. Every so often, a cicada or an engine could be heard in the distance. The drizzle pattered on the roof. A far-off dog howled. The stars in the sky disappeared, and everything seemed to go black.

—

Shivering from the cold, the crazy woman tried to move away from the water, but Scarface shoved her body back into place with one kick. After holding her there with his boot for a few more moments, Scarface finally bent over and with nimble movements stripped Scarlet Blush of her clothes. He even ripped off her bra, and maneuvered her legs so he could pull down her underwear.

"You're a disgusting crazy woman!" he insulted her.

But after that he turned quite gentle. He took some soap and shampoo, and he washed Scarlet Blush. She tried to run out of the bathroom a few times, but Scarface pushed her back under the faucet easily.

"Stay still, psycho. I've never been this nice to anybody. I've never bathed my wife and when my mother died, I didn't bathe her corpse. I've never even given my own kid a bath. As long as I've lived, I've only ever bathed my commander's water buffalo and you, so stay still. Really, you should thank me. You'll sleep better with a clean body. There's no point in being dirty and smelly."

He even forced her to open her mouth and brushed her teeth for her.

"Show me that grin! Now that's good. Your teeth are nice and straight, they look attractive now that they're clean."

—

Ajo Kawir pressed himself tighter against the wall of the house, trying to avoid the drizzle. He looked over at Gecko, with his eyes asking is-a-view-like-this-really-so-interesting? Gecko answered him with a look that said just-wait-you-are-always-so-impatient.

The mosquitos buzzed and hummed. Mosquitos and drizzle. Ajo Kawir was truly fed up and looked over at Gecko repeatedly, always with the same expression. But Gecko ignored him and kept his eyes glued to his peephole. Ajo Kawir grew even more annoyed, but peeked into the house again. He gave up trying to kick the mosquitos off his calves, and just let them drink his blood to their heart's content.

—

The Clove Smoker was still sucking on his cigarette, letting the ash fall onto the floor. He lifted his other leg, and rested it on top of the leg that was leaning on the wall. He twirled his clove cigarette expertly; the ember never once grazed his skin. After a bit of that, he began to whistle.

Tired of whistling, he began to sing softly in an off-key voice. It sounded like a Malaysian song from the sixties, maybe one by P. Ramlee. He looked very bored but there was not much else he could do to kill the time. He yawned. He took another drag on his cigarette and exhaled the smoke toward the ceiling.

Then he threw the butt onto the floor, crushed it with his boot, and stood up. He paced back and forth and then took a broom and swept up the butt and the ash. Then he cleaned what was left of the crumbs of Scarlet Blush's meal. He even gathered up the dirty dishes and brought them to the kitchen. He didn't wash them, but at least he put them aside. Then he returned to the main room and began organizing the randomly scattered chairs.

Soon he went back to sit in the corner. He took out another clove, lit it, and rested both his legs against the wall once again.

Scarface dragged Scarlet Blush back out of the bathroom, water dripping off her body. Her breasts quivered as she stumbled into the middle of the room. The floor all around her was now wet too. Scarface pushed Scarlet Blush down into a chair not far from the table and she sat there, shivering.

Scarface went into the kitchen and came back out carrying a towel. He dried the woman's hair. The crazy lady just sat there without responding. Scarface gently dried her off. He dried her wet cheeks. Dried her breasts. Dried her armpits, her back, her thighs, and her ass. Scarlet Blush did nothing.

"It's really such a pity that this woman is crazy."

"There you go again. It's not a pity."

"It is."

Scarlet Blush was dry now. Scarface approached her, stood behind her, and wrapped his arms around her. He slowly rubbed her breasts. Scarface's hands moved like a potter molding wet clay, making circles that followed her curves. Scarlet Blush moaned. Scarface sniffed the crown of the woman's head as his caresses grew more insistent. The Clove Smoker glanced in their direction every once in a while, but mostly stayed unmoving on his chair.

Scarface looked over at his friend. Then he lifted up Scarlet Blush's body. She tried to sit back down again but he forced her to stand and pushed her toward the table, pressing her flat on her back. And so there Scarlet Blush was, naked on the table like an evening meal. She tried to curl up and cross her legs, but Scarface forced them open again.

—

Gecko looked over at Ajo Kawir. The kid seemed to be readjusting something inside his shorts. Gecko smiled. He knew that Ajo Kawir's dick must be getting big.

"I didn't know she was this pretty," Ajo Kawir whispered.

"You just have to give her a bath."

"I like her more than the headman's wife."

"But his wife's boobs are as big as young coconuts."

"Hers are better. They're not as big, but they're really good."

"What did I tell you?"

Ajo Kawir almost missed an important sight: Scarface had taken off his shoes and his pants, showing his black ass scarred with boils and his genitals that were almost hidden behind a thick patch of hair that hadn't been trimmed in who knows how long. Scarface was getting ready to climb up on to the table, pushing Scarlet Blush back down onto her back. Spreading her legs.

Suddenly, Scarlet Blush shoved Scarface and tried to get away. Scarface reeled back, but he caught Scarlet Blush and pinned her to the table. Scarlet Blush fought him off but Scarface climbed up and crushed her under his weight. She let out a little shriek and Scarface slapped her face yelling, "Shut up, psycho!"

Greedily, Scarface went back to licking Scarlet Blush's breasts, burying his face in them while the woman thrashed about.

The village headman puts his thing in his wife's cleavage, thought Ajo Kawir, while this policeman buries his face in Scarlet Blush's. He wondered, out of the two of those, which one felt better? He wanted to talk this over with Gecko, but not right now. He didn't want to miss anything important.

Scarface picked up one of Scarlet Blush's legs and placed it over his shoulder. He was ready to bury himself inside the woman, and would have done it, if something hadn't happened.

Ajo Kawir, watching the unfolding scene and shivering, never once moving his eyes from the peephole, lost his grip on the windowsill, and before he could catch himself, he slipped. The sound of him crashing to the ground startled everyone.

Gecko leapt into the bushes and the Clove Smoker jumped up from his chair. Ajo Kawir was still trying to scramble up when he was seized by the smoker, who was already at his side.

A minute later Ajo Kawir was standing next to the table where Scarlet Blush was still lying naked on her back. The Clove Smoker was holding him firmly.

"Is this what you wanted to see, kid?" Scarface demanded.

Ajo Kawir, terrified, shook his head and tried to get away. But the Clove Smoker took out his pistol and, putting it to the boy's head, ordered, "Stay still and watch!"

The muzzle felt cold against his skin and out of the corner of his eye, he could see the pistol shining. And that was how, with his body trembling violently, this time from fear, with a pale face and quivering lips, unable to make a sound, Ajo Kawir was forced to watch those two soldiers take turns raping Scarlet Blush.

—

Gecko, who at first didn't know what had happened, came out of the bushes and crept back to the window. From there he saw Ajo Kawir, standing like a living corpse beside the table. Gecko wondered whether he should go inside and help Ajo Kawir, but when he saw the pistol that was pressed to his friend's head, he stayed put, overwhelmed. The thought crossed his mind to go tell someone what was going on, but after he mulled it over for a moment, he decided that the whole mess would just get more complicated if he did, and made up his mind to wait.

The worst part was yet to come. After they put their pants back on, the two policemen looked at Ajo Kawir. Scarface suddenly grinned in his direction and asked, "You want to try?"

Ajo Kawir shook his head weakly, practically collapsing.

The Clove Smoker pointed his pistol at the boy again and barked, "Take off your pants!"

Ajo Kawir didn't move. He felt the pistol's ice-cold muzzle on his forehead, sending a chill throughout his body once again.

Scarface impatiently ripped off Ajo Kawir's clothes, until the boy was naked, and pushed him toward Scarlet Blush, still naked on the dining table. Ajo Kawir staggered forward and stopped right in front of Scarlet Blush's legs, spread wide. Behind her pubic hair, Ajo Kawir saw the reddish folds and crack.

"Put it in!"

Ajo Kawir didn't move. The two policemen were annoyed and were about to take his pecker in their own hands to force it into the woman, but then, looking down at Ajo Kawir's crotch, they fell silent. They never would have predicted it, but the boy's penis was curled up as small as it could get, shriveled and practically collapsed in on itself. After staring for a moment, the two policemen burst out laughing, slapping the table.

"You useless kid! Even a dog would get horny seeing a woman like this."

—

The good thing was that they let him go immediately and ordered him to leave. The bad thing was, ever since that day, Ajo Kawir's dick could not stand up. It wouldn't have stood up even if there had been twelve naked whores in front of him, and they had tried every trick in the book to get it up for him.

And not long after that night, the people found Scarlet Blush dead in her own backyard. Lying there next to her husband's grave.

❋2❋

AJO KAWIR WENT to the kitchen and found some red chili peppers sitting among the spices. He looked into the main room. Nobody was around. I'm acting like a common thief, he thought. He first took a few peppers but then decided on just the plumpest, freshest-looking one. It was red, tinged with green. He chopped off its tip with a knife. He could see the seeds inside, white and oozing. It would be delicious with shrimp crackers or hot fried tempeh, he thought. But he didn't have any shrimp crackers or fried tempeh, and this wasn't the time to think about food. He peered around again—the house was still deserted. He looked back at the chili pepper.

Ajo Kawir unzipped his jeans and pulled down his underwear. His pecker was hanging there, still sleeping, as lazy as could be.

If you don't want to get up, he thought, then I will make you get up.

He rubbed the chopped chili pepper across the surface of his genitals, making lines and circles. He cut a bit more off the chili and rubbed again. Get up, he mumbled. Get up, you deadbeat. He had already applied the chili pepper to the entire surface of his privates and the seeds were sticking here and there, like sesame seeds. At first it just felt cold, a very suspicious cold.

But after a while, it began to feel warm. And then hot. And then it began to sting.

He started howling in the kitchen, and then he moved to the bathroom, yelling and screaming, until his voice could be heard eleven houses away. They found him there, soaked to the bone. He was dousing his crotch with pail after pail of water, howling and screaming and flailing about.

"It burns! It burns!"

"Of course it burns, you idiot!"

There was nothing anyone could do. They dragged him from the bathroom and gave him a towel and left him to scream on his bed. He rolled back and forth on the mattress. He wept. His tears poured onto his red face. People wanted to laugh at him, but nobody did. Or at least, they laughed later when he wasn't around. Nobody knew where he had gotten the idea, but one thing was clear: chili peppers would not make your dick stand up. They wouldn't even make it twitch. All they'd do was make it red, and make its owner suffer for practically half the day.

—

"Unbelievably stupid," Gecko pronounced two days later. He had once accidentally dribbled some toothpaste out of his mouth onto his privates and the heat had been merciless. He couldn't even imagine what a red chili pepper must feel like—he'd never be that dumb.

"But I have to try whatever I can," Ajo Kawir explained, "to save my own life."

You idiot, Gecko grumbled in reply, your soul doesn't reside in your penis.

At that time, nobody knew that his dick couldn't stand up except Gecko. Of course, people wondered why he had done something so ridiculous, but he didn't tell them anything. They thought maybe Ajo Kawir had heard some mistaken advice about virility. Kids these days wanted a penis that was strong and big, and they'd try anything to get one, without even knowing with whom they'd ever put it to use—boys just thought that a big strong penis was the best thing that they could ever have.

No, people didn't know yet that Ajo Kawir's dick couldn't stand up.

—

Gecko wondered whether he should tell his father about it or not. Someone has to know, he thought. Someone has to help Ajo Kawir. He looked at Iwan Angsa, feeding his hen and her nine chicks in the side yard. It was morning and he was carrying his school bag but finally he decided to talk to his father. He approached a bit hesitantly and then stood behind Iwan Angsa, watching him stir the wet bran before giving it to the chicken, who'd share it with her chicks.

"What is it?" asked Iwan Angsa when he saw his son hovering there. "Do you want some money?"

"No."

"So why haven't you left yet?"

He wondered whether he should say anything. He looked at his father. He thought of Ajo Kawir. If he was going to tell, what exactly should he say? Iwan Angsa returned his gaze for a few moments. The chickens were waiting and he gave them another spoonful of wet bran. Gecko still just stood there with his busy thoughts. Finally, he said:

"Ajo Kawir's dick can't stand up."

Iwan Angsa looked at him in confusion. "What do you mean?"

"Ajo Kawir's pecker can't stand up. Even if he's looking at a naked woman, it doesn't stand up. The thing is, it won't stand up, no matter what."

—

Not far from their house, there was a farmer who was trying to keep bees. Gecko would go there to buy honey. It wasn't very good honey, and the farmer knew it, he just did it because he enjoyed it. And Ajo Kawir had gone there once with Gecko, and a bee had stung him, making his hand swell up.

Then he read something about bee therapy in an old newspaper. Bee stings could cure all kinds of illnesses, the article said. Beriberi, rheumatism, gout. He didn't know what those illnesses were, but he knew that a bee sting could make his hand swell up.

Ajo Kawir thought about his penis. He imagined it getting bigger. Standing up. Erect.

He went to the farmer and bought a bottle of honey, and asked for a few bees too, although he didn't say for what. He went home and purposefully let his penis get stung three times. And it did in fact get bigger, it swelled almost as wide as his fist, but it could not be considered erect. You could say it was more like a sleeping python. And so he was left to howl and moan for the second time, and he couldn't wear pants for the rest of the afternoon.

—

A few days later Gecko brought the subject up again with Iwan Angsa. He was on the verge of tears as he spoke. "Dad, you have to do something," he begged.

"But what's really wrong with it, exactly?"

"I already told you, Ajo Kawir's dick can't stand up. Even if he sees a naked lady it can't. He already tried rubbing it with a red chili pepper, and now he's let bees sting it, but he still can't get hard."

"What do you guys know about dicks, anyway?"

—

Iwan Angsa brought Ajo Kawir into his room, and told him to take off his pants. Ajo Kawir sat on the edge of the bed, his eyes welling up. Iwan Angsa squatted and examined it. Pinched it and tweaked it. Ajo Kawir wiped away his tears, and begged that no one tell his mother or his father. He didn't want them to know about this.

"But how did it all start?" Iwan Angsa asked.

Ajo Kawir looked over at Gecko. Gecko looked back at him. We don't know, Gecko blurted out. He didn't want Iwan Angsa to know what they'd done. He didn't want to add on to all their problems. He didn't want to talk about how the two policemen had gone into Scarlet Blush's house, and raped that crazy woman. We just don't know, he said again.

Iwan Angsa looked at Ajo Kawir.

"I don't know," Ajo Kawir repeated. "All of a sudden, it just didn't want to stand up. But it used to stand up, like if I was looking at a picture of a half-naked lady."

"Or if he rubbed it with soap," Gecko added.

Iwan Angsa gave him some thin adult books by Valentino, which he occasionally bought for himself at the bus terminal. He had a few stashed away in a locked cupboard in his bedroom. He hadn't wanted the kids to find them, but now he gave them to Ajo Kawir and told him to read up. They were about nothing but intercourse, filled with the snorts of lusty women and the howls of men in orgasm. Sometimes there were sepia photographs of people doing it slipped in between the pages, or of women showing off their genitals.

Iwan Angsa had read those books again and again as enter-tainment before getting into bed and waiting for Wa Sami. Those books were always able to make his dick hard, sometimes even until he came. And now he hoped those books would offer that same miraculous gift to Ajo Kawir.

He left the kid to read the books in his room. Ajo Kawir sat on the edge of the mattress just like before, but this time without wear-ing any pants. His hands were busy flipping through the pages. Of course he really enjoyed them—there's no one who doesn't enjoy a book like that.

Every couple of minutes, Iwan Angsa would spy on the kid through the air vent above the door.

"How's it going?" asked Gecko, waiting nearby.

Iwan Angsa didn't say anything. He saw that Ajo Kawir was still sitting there on the edge of the mattress. He had already read four books. And his penis was still sleeping soundly, looking exactly like a lump of ginger root.

—

It was past eleven o'clock at night. Iwan Angsa was leading Ajo Kawir along a footpath that stretched out next to the railroad tracks. Only a pale streetlight lit their way. They arrived at a place with small huts and a few people visible in silhouette sitting on narrow benches. There was dim light from a small five-watt light bulb and the oil lamp of a fried snack seller who had set up at the roadside.

They stopped at one of the huts, which appeared abandoned. Iwan Angsa looked around. Ajo Kawir's hand felt cold in his. He looked down at the boy. Ajo Kawir seemed uncomfortable, and whispered that he wanted to leave, but Iwan Angsa held him there without replying.

A woman appeared out of the darkness and approached them.

Standing in front of the two of them, she asked, "Looking for something sweet?"

"Yeah, I need a woman for this kid."

She looked at Ajo Kawir and smiled—almost laughed, really. She held out her hand to Ajo Kawir but the kid just clasped Iwan Angsa's hand tighter. Come here, said the woman, and I'll teach you a thing or two, just like we taught your dad here. Iwan Angsa was going to say that the boy wasn't his son, but decided not to mention it.

Instead he said, "I want you to make his dick stand up. Whatever it takes."

"Well of course. That's what I'm paid to do."

If before he was clutching Iwan Angsa's hand tight, now Ajo Kawir tried to escape from his grip. Iwan Angsa didn't let him go, just watched the kid as he tried to break free with all his might. Iwan Angsa shook his head and pushed him toward the door of the hut. The woman opened the door and went in. There was the light of a different lamp inside the hut. Iwan Angsa dragged Ajo Kawir inside, and left him there, going back outside and closing the door.

He sat down on the track and caught sight of someone he knew. The men took out their clove cigarettes and chatted.

—

When Iwan Angsa decided to take Ajo Kawir out, Gecko asked to join, but Iwan Angsa forbade him, saying it was grown-up business. But Ajo Kawir is still a teenager, Gecko protested, I'm the same age as him. Iwan Angsa still wouldn't let him come. Ajo Kawir and Gecko were different—as different as life and death, or as a dick that can stand up and one that can't. Wait at the house and don't go anywhere, Iwan Angsa said.

But secretly, Gecko followed them—lucky for him they walked, so it was easy. He trailed them almost to the tracks, where he saw a woman approach them, and soon after that he saw them disappear into a hut. Ajo Kawir was in that hut with that woman. Gecko decided to find out what was going on inside.

Through a crack in the wall, Gecko could clearly see the prostitute trying every way she knew to make her mission succeed. She took Ajo Kawir's clothes off, and then took her own clothes off. She fondled Ajo Kawir's genitals. Ajo Kawir didn't do anything, and neither did his dick. The prostitute moved her lips close to it, opening her mouth to show a gaping row of sharp pointy teeth, and Gecko almost shrieked because for a moment he thought the prostitute was going to eat Ajo Kawir's privates. He remembered the pussy with teeth. But of course the woman didn't bite into it.

"This has never happened in my entire life," she said in a tone of annoyance.

She grabbed the kid's torso and positioned him over her, trying to bury his cock inside her own body. She shook her hips. She made a seductive face. But nothing about the kid's genitals changed. Finally she stopped, and looked at him in defeat.

"There is nothing more demeaning to a prostitute than a bird that won't stand up."

All her efforts had taken about an hour, and Iwan Angsa finally came in, telling them to put their clothes back on.

Iwan Angsa led the kid away from the railroad tracks. At first, he didn't say anything. Ajo Kawir didn't say anything. Trailing behind them in secret, Gecko didn't say anything either.

Then, with a sad face, Iwan Angsa finally spoke. "Nothing can help you."

Gecko walked faster, taking a shortcut to get back to the house first—he didn't want to get in trouble with his father.

—

One morning, with fog still hanging in the air, Gecko was hungry and Wa Sami hadn't cooked anything. She said, buy something out. He wanted to find a pancake seller before bathing and leaving for school and set out walking past the back of Ajo Kawir's house.

He saw the boy standing in front of a woodpile, the place where his father usually chopped firewood. In addition to being a librarian, his father also had a small brick-making business, and the oven wasn't far from their house. And there Ajo Kawir was, where the wood was usually chopped to stoke the mud kiln, with his pants sagging down and his tanned buttocks visible. Gecko was intrigued, and turned around to take a closer look. He saw Ajo Kawir placing his penis on the chopping block, his right hand lifting a hatchet high in the air, undoubtedly intending to hack off the little hunk of lazy flesh hanging from his crotch.

Gecko sprang into action and lunged for the hatchet. Ajo Kawir, surprised, tried to free himself from Gecko's clutches. Knowing that this struggle might go on for a while if he didn't act fast, Gecko socked Ajo Kawir right on the nose. Ajo Kawir was stunned and Gecko was able to wrench the hatchet away.

"You dope! What are you doing?"

Ajo Kawir didn't answer. He hiked his pants back up, hiding his genitals away. Then he sat down and his eyes welled up with tears. Gecko thought to himself that ever since Ajo Kawir's dick stopped standing up, he'd become a bit of a crybaby.

Even though he wasn't sure about it at all, Gecko tried to comfort his friend: "At some point, your bird will definitely stand up again. You'd better believe it. And hey, even if it could stand up now, come on, who would you even use it with?"

The question made Ajo Kawir look over. He wiped his wet eyes, and then gave a little smile. That little smile became a wide grin, which then turned into a chuckle.

Gecko laughed too.

"You're right, even if it could stand up now, who'd want it?"

Ajo Kawir laughed again, and Gecko laughed with him. That morning, they laughed together. People walking by peered at them, but they just kept laughing and so the passersby just wrinkled their foreheads and frowned.

Gecko brought Ajo Kawir to the pancake stall and bought him a snack.

—

After that Ajo Kawir was fine, or at least Gecko thought so. There were no signs that he was still lamenting his inability to get erect, nor were there any more indications of despair. As a friend, Gecko tried to keep Ajo Kawir happy, or at the very least prevent him from dwelling on his unfortunate fate or what had occurred at Scarlet Blush's house.

Years passed and nothing else happened. They went to school. They caused trouble. They got into fights on the streets, in the movie theater, at the swimming pool, and on the soccer field.

They got kicked out of school, were reenrolled by Iwan Angsa, and then got kicked out again. They lived their lives. They both had sad lives, scraping by at the bottom, but they were happy. Or they pretended to be happy. Or at least they tried to learn how to be happy.

—

Until a problem arose.

One day, far in the future, Ajo Kawir would meet a woman named Jelita. But before that happened, when he was nineteen years old, he met a girl. Her name was Iteung. And that girl fell in love with Ajo Kawir.

—

Ajo Kawir was sitting in Wa Sami's shop when a girl came in. He knew her. She was his classmate, Rani. They exchanged greetings. What's new, Rani, where are you living now? Rani was continuing her schooling at the university in Bandung. Ajo Kawir said that he wasn't going anywhere. He had just gotten kicked out of school for the however-many-eth time, he had lost track, and Iwan Angsa was trying to convince the principal to let him back in. Meanwhile, he was helping Wa Sami look after the store. Same thing with Gecko, but he was out somewhere, maybe hauling sacks of rice.

Rani sat on the store's front patio with Ajo Kawir. She filled him in on what had happened since the last time they met. She told him about what was going on with their friends. Then she told him about a woman who had been living at her house for the past few weeks. Rani had come to the shop to buy milk for the child of this woman, who was called the Young Widow because she didn't want to say her name.

She was a young widow, about thirty-two years old, with two children. She rented a house from a guy in the fishpond business. "Do you know Mister Lebe? No? That's okay. That's the name of the fishpond guy." Before he died, her husband was a musician in an *angklung* performance troupe. They'd been on some national TV shows and were invited to perform every time a provincial or central official came to visit.

"But don't think that because they were on television that they made a lot of money," Rani said.

The Young Widow's husband had died about six months ago, and she'd been left with no savings, no inheritance, and don't even ask about life insurance.

The Young Widow didn't have a job either, or any relatives. This whole time she'd kept busy taking care of her two small children, the oldest one had just turned three. She began to sell the things she had around the house to survive. She had come to Rani's house to sell her black-and-white television, and Rani's father had bought it out of pity. She also sold her radio. Then she sold her table and her old chair. She sold whatever she could sell. She approached all her neighbors, hoping they might want to buy whatever she had.

—

Two months after her husband died, Mister Lebe, the fishpond man, came to collect the rent.

"How are you going to pay your rent on this house?"

"Wait a bit, Sir. I don't have any money right now."

"So when are you going to get some money?"

The woman fell silent. She just bit her lip. She didn't dare meet Mister Lebe's eyes. She rolled and unrolled the hem of her shirt. She hoped that God would send her down some money at that very moment and all of her troubles would end. She stayed quiet, not knowing what to say.

"Actually, you don't have to pay rent," Mister Lebe said.

"What do you mean?" She gathered the courage to lift her face and look at the man, hoping Mister Lebe had taken pity on her.

"You know, I want to sleep in your room sometimes. If you let me, you don't have to pay your rent. You can live here for as long as you want."

"Sir?"

"Of course, I wouldn't just be sleeping in your room. I'd want you to keep me company."

The little mouth grinning beneath his thin mustache reminded the Young Widow of a rat's snout.

—

She lay on the bed and cried. Mister Lebe had already taken off his clothes. She hoped that she wouldn't have to see him, but he touched her face and made her look at him. She cried some more and Mister Lebe smiled.

"Come on, don't cry. If you cry it won't feel good. It won't be juicy."

Mister Lebe got on top of her, probing every curve and crevice of her body. She kept on crying. Mister Lebe traced the outline of her lips, caressing her neck and her ears. She wept.

"I won't just let you live here—I'll make sure that you and your children never go hungry."

Mister Lebe opened her legs. He entered her. She closed her eyes tight, but tears still streamed out from the cracks of her eyelids. She felt pain. Not just down there, but deep in her chest.

—

"What a son of a bitch!" Ajo Kawir swore. "I've never liked men like that. A man like that should be hung, and his corpse dragged along the road for all to see. And his dick should be shredded to bits."

"That sounds like a great idea," Rani said. "But no one would dare lay a hand on Mister Lebe. He's a close friend of the District Head. And he's protected by all the local thugs."

—

And that was how the fishpond guy could come at any time—sometimes he'd let her know beforehand, and other times he just showed up and brought the Young Widow to the bed, leaving her with a pain in her privates and her chest.

As bad as it was, the Young Widow was patient with the situation. She accepted her landlord's unpredictable visits. But after a while, he began to bring his friends. At first he just brought one, but then he brought somebody different, and then another day he brought two at once. At first the Young Widow refused to service them, but her landlord threatened to drag her and the two children out of the house and toss them in the street. She had no choice, so she received them all on her bed.

The pain in her chest grew deeper and wider. She no longer cared about the other pain.

Then misfortune befell her: she got pregnant. She didn't know who the baby's father was. Her only option was to ask her landlord to take responsibility. If he wouldn't marry her, then perhaps he'd at least take care of the baby. But instead he got angry and kicked her out. And that was how she came to tell her harrowing tale to the young girl of the family who was sheltering her for the moment: Rani.

—

Ajo Kawir was immediately reminded of Scarlet Blush, and all her suffering, and all the suffering that he himself had to bear.

"I don't have a lot of money, but sometimes I save up a little bit for a rainy day. I'll go get it. Give my money to this Young Widow."

"Are you serious?" asked Rani.

"Of course. Maybe she can use the money to terminate her pregnancy if she wants. Or to take care of the kid."

—

The woman decided to terminate the pregnancy. She managed to get additional donations from some other folks, even though it didn't add up to much. Rani explained that her life wasn't even as easy as she'd first said. Most people sneered at her, both women and men. Only Rani's family would accept her, and so that's where the woman was hiding. Hearing all that from Ajo Kawir, Gecko convinced Wa Sami to chip in a little money.

But it turned out that the story didn't end there. A few days later, the fishpond guy reported the Young Widow to the police, accusing her of slandering him just so she could avoid having to pay her rent. The woman was called to the station and had to undergo an exhausting interrogation. Everyone knew that the odds were stacked against her. She didn't have a witness for anything she'd said, and even if she could find the remains of her terminated pregnancy, there was no guarantee that the child belonged to the fishpond guy. People gossiped that—after she'd sold everything else she had—the woman had knowingly sold herself.

—

"I feel like I have to kill this asshole—what's his name? Mister Lebe? He's going to become my first murder victim," Ajo Kawir said. "I like to fight, I miss fighting. I would gladly take his life."

"Don't be stupid," Rani said.

Rani was sure that Ajo Kawir would never actually do anything so foolish.

Gecko tried to dissuade him, saying that it'd be a dumb thing to do.

"Iwan Angsa has said that the world isn't fair," Ajo Kawir replied, "And that if we find a way to make it more fair, then we should make it fair."

"I just don't want you to get beaten to a bloody pulp and die in ridiculous agony," Gecko said. "I heard these businessmen hire guys from the Empty Hand."

Everyone knew businessmen kept thugs. But the members of the Empty Hand weren't typical petty criminals. Not much was known about the group. If anyone had heard of them, they just thought they were a typical gang of bad kids going around causing trouble—some of them had ties to the police, but others had been arrested for fighting with rival gangs. What most people didn't know was that, if they killed someone, yes, sometimes it was just a typical street fight, but more often than not, they'd been paid to do it. And despite their name, they were devious masters of all kinds of weapons.

"They could stab you in the back while you're walking down some deserted back alley."

"I'm not scared of them."

—

The fishpond businessman of course owned his own fishpond, a place he often went to be alone. Whatever his reasons for going there, the pond—with its small bungalows and the gardens all around—struck Ajo Kawir as the perfect spot for an ambush.

So he went there, but what he didn't know was that the man had a bodyguard—a young woman, who intercepted him on the footpath. And this was how he met Iteung.

—

"I know you've been eyeing that old fart, I've been watching you," the girl said. "But you'll have to kill me before you can lay a hand on him."

Ajo Kawir almost laughed at her choice of words, copied verbatim from the martial arts comics that he'd read when he was little, borrowed from the librarian who went around on his bicycle. He had never hit a woman, so he just shoved Iteung aside. Unexpectedly, the girl grabbed his arm and pinned it behind his back, and with just a little push threw him to the ground, pummeling his shoulders.

Shocked, Ajo Kawir jumped up, although he staggered a bit. Iteung put up her fists. Ajo Kawir didn't know what the girl had studied—maybe karate, silat, kempo, or kung fu—but he didn't know any of that stuff anyway. He just knew to punch and kick when he had the opportunity, dodge whenever possible. If he couldn't dodge, then he would take the hit and look for a way to retaliate.

"Fine," said Ajo Kawir. "I guess every once in a while you have to fight a woman."

And that afternoon, they fought. Iteung had clearly mastered the martial arts. Despite her delicate looks, she was very strong and had good stamina. Ajo Kawir took hit after solid hit, and he had to admit to himself that her powerful blows hurt more than the punches most men threw.

Even though he'd never studied any kind of martial arts, Ajo Kawir was no easy conquest. He was strong and, above all, reckless. Even when cornered, he was the kind of fighter who'd let his opponent break his arm if it gave him the opportunity to break the other guy's leg. That killer instinct made it hard for the girl to take him down, even though she struck him again and again, suffering punches and kicks in return.

More than an hour passed as they knocked each other around, landing blows. Ajo Kawir's cheek was split open, the girl's nose was dripping blood, and their bruises—don't even ask. Finally exhausted, Ajo Kawir could do nothing but throw weak punches at the girl's face, which Iteung easily blocked with equally weak fists, until they both collapsed in the grass, gasping for breath.

"Not bad," Iteung murmured faintly a few moments later, barely audible in the rushing wind.

"Damn," said Ajo Kawir. "I can still take you."

"Forget it. You should just go home. Who sent you here? You don't need to get mixed up with people like this."

"Nobody sent me. I came on my own."

"I don't believe you."

"You don't have to. I came because I heard about what he did to that woman."

"Which one? The Young Widow?"

"Yeah."

Iteung gave a small nod. Collapsed there in the grass, beside the garden footpath, they were lying on their backs looking up at the sky. They were silent for a moment, perhaps both thinking about the Young Widow. Finally the girl rolled over onto her side, and looked at Ajo Kawir.

"Do you want to know the real story?"

"What is it?"

—

One night, Mister Lebe came to see the Young Widow, although at that time she wasn't yet a widow. It was almost eleven o'clock. He said that he was just stopping by to check in on the house. The Young Widow couldn't refuse to let him in, because even though they'd paid their rent, it was his house.

"Where's your husband?" asked Mister Lebe.

"He's practicing *angklung*, getting ready for a show."

Mister Lebe actually knew that without having to ask, since her husband often returned from his rehearsals late at night when he was preparing for a performance. He smiled and looked at the woman before him.

"You're not lonely?"

"What do you mean?"

"Your husband always comes home so late," Mister Lebe said. He smiled again and the Young Widow thought that underneath his thin mustache, it was the most disgusting smile she'd ever seen. "You must be lonely. I can keep you company if you want."

"I'm not lonely."

"But I'm lonely," said Mister Lebe. "And sometimes I imagine that you want to keep me company."

"I'm not lonely. If you are feeling lonely, then you should hurry home to spend some time with your wife." She wanted to spit in his face, but she controlled herself.

—

"That woman had no reason to betray her husband, because she loved him. But then that old carcass murdered the musician," Iteung said.

"Murdered?"

"Lots of people thought he died of cholera, because he was vomiting and had diarrhea one night at a party after a performance. But in fact, it was poison. The woman doesn't even know that her husband was murdered. After that, well, you know the rest."

"How do you know all this?"

"I know who killed him. Someone from the Empty Hand— Mister Lebe paid him to do it."

"The bastard!"

—

They were still lying in the grass. Ajo Kawir's body felt completely broken. He looked up at the sky, and saw a hawk soaring in the distance. He tried to raise his arm, but he had no energy left. He looked to the side and the girl was looking back. For a moment, their eyes locked. Feeling a bit shy, Ajo Kawir looked back up at the sky.

"If you can still stand, go see that old carcass. I have some Chinese medicine in my bag. My teacher at the academy gave it to me. You'll recover in fifteen minutes, but then in six hours you'll collapse again and you won't be able to get up for three days. So do whatever you came here to do, quickly." Ajo Kawir looked back at the girl. "But don't kill him, that would make things difficult," said Iteung, "for the woman."

Ajo Kawir didn't move or say anything. But he ground his teeth together, and his fists clenched.

"Oh, and cover your face, you idiot." The girl smiled in his direction.

Ajo Kawir saw her bag in a corner of the garden. He looked back at the girl and only then did he realize how pretty she was, especially when she smiled. That smile momentarily quieted his anger. After she nodded, Ajo Kawir crawled with great difficulty toward the bag. He found a face mask inside, some black cloth, and the medicine—Ajo Kawir offered some to Iteung, but she shook her head.

"You know I don't need it."

—

He found Mister Lebe feeding his fish in the pond.

"Good afternoon, Sir, there's something I need to discuss with you."

He wasn't wearing the mask, because he didn't think it was necessary. Mister Lebe didn't know him, but he escorted him into his small bungalow. "What brings you here?" Mr. Lebe asked while offering Ajo Kawir a seat.

But the kid felt no need to sit down first—in fact, he felt their small talk had already gone on for too long. "This is what brings me here!" he cried as he threw a punch at Mister Lebe's face.

"Hey, who are you?"

"I'm a demon from hell," Ajo Kawir said, kicking the old guy in the crotch.

Mister Lebe stumbled, but before he fell to the floor, Ajo Kawir had already hit him again. One, two, three, solid punches. Mister Lebe couldn't do anything except holler.

"Iteung! Iteung!"

"There's no point in calling for her. She's out there dying in your garden."

He threw one more punch and Mister Lebe slammed back against the wall, collapsing, his cheek split open. He was starting to wheeze. Blood was streaming out from his nose. Ajo Kawir stretched out his fingers and then squatted down next to Mister Lebe.

"Don't you dare bother the Young Widow ever again, because if you do, I'll be back, and next time, I'll kill you. I'm not playing around. Remember my face, if you think you can mess with me."

"Yeah, yeah, okay. No, no, I won't mess with you."

"And as a sign of our agreement, I'd like something from you."

Ajo Kawir took out a pocketknife, grabbed Mister Lebe's left ear and sliced it off, and the man's howls rang out over the farthest reaches of his fishpond.

—

Ajo Kawir stood at the edge of the pond. Mister Lebe's howls could no longer be heard, because he had fainted. Ajo Kawir threw the man's ear into the pond. A fish jumped up and caught it. Maybe it was a goldfish, or a carp, or a catfish. They're really all the same.

—

Just as the girl had said, he woke up three days later. He'd gone to sleep at Gecko's house, because he knew only Gecko would stay by his side for three days and three nights. That day the house telephone—or, more accurately, Wa Sami's store telephone—rang, and someone asked for Ajo Kawir. Wa Sami handed the telephone to him, and bemused, he took it.

"So, how'd you sleep? I hope you're doing all right."

It was a girl's voice. He didn't immediately recognize the caller, and he had no idea how anyone knew that he was at Gecko's house. But then he realized—it was the girl who had dueled with him. Iteung. He smiled. He hadn't grinned so widely in years.

—

After that, they sent each other short messages through the radio. Morning, noon, and night. Gecko witnessed an incredible change in Ajo Kawir. He'd sit for hours by the radio, listening and dedicating songs to a girl, with a little smile playing across his shining face. Gecko didn't have to ask, he immediately knew which girl Ajo Kawir liked. It was enough to make him feel overjoyed too.

After dozens, or maybe even more than a hundred songs dedicated to each other on the radio, they met at a restaurant and then went to the City Festival, which was held every August. To make sure they were all right, they examined each other's scars, and then they both laughed. The girl wasn't just pretty, thought Ajo Kawir, she was also a lot of fun. From her Ajo Kawir learned that the rotten old fishpond guy had entrusted his business to a family member and had vanished; or, more accurately, his wife had kicked him out.

—

Not long after that, Ajo Kawir also learned that Iteung often worked for the Empty Hand. She wasn't a member of the group—the Empty Hand only accepted men—but she knew one gang member, who'd been in her class at the martial arts academy. Sometimes, if the group had work guarding someone and their members were already busy, they'd offer Iteung the job.

"You're an incredible fighter," said Ajo Kawir.

"Of course. And you're an amazing sand bag," Iteung said, chuckling.

They walked through the festival, buying balloons and sweets, laughing. Then, while they were walking, Iteung took Ajo Kawir's hand, as if asking to continue along as a couple. Warmth spread throughout his chest.

Ajo Kawir looked over at the girl. She looked over at him. They smiled, and they giggled. A tinge of red flushed the girl's cheeks. Iteung bowed her head.

Ajo Kawir felt happy. So very happy. And he also felt afraid ...

—

Quietly, Gecko observed all of that, and also this part:

One Saturday night, in a deserted parking lot, Ajo Kawir and Iteung were pressed together, leaning against a wall. They were kissing. Gecko thought that maybe this was the first time Ajo Kawir had ever kissed a girl, with smoldering kisses that never seemed to end.

The girl took Ajo Kawir's hand, guided it under her shirt, and placed it on her breast. That gave Ajo Kawir goose bumps, excited and nervous. He squeezed the girl's chest, and Iteung shivered. Their temperatures began to rise.

With racing breath, one of Iteung's hands slipped into Ajo Kawir's pants. He realized this, and quickly caught her wrist and gently moved it away from his button fly.

He knew that her hand would come back, and felt he had to do something before that happened. So while his left hand kept caressing the girl's breasts, his right hand descended and then reached up under Iteung's skirt, slipping into her underwear. Who knows where he learned how, but his middle finger crept and found a crack. The girl was already wet. His middle finger kept exploring the crack until he found a curve and a small bulge. His finger slowly burrowed in, investigating.

The girl felt like she was floating, and she grunted before letting out a little cry and drooping onto Ajo Kawir's shoulder. Then they both slid down and sat, leaning against the wall.

"Thank you," said Iteung. "I haven't given you yours."

"Some other time." Ajo Kawir's voice sounded uncertain.

—

Ajo Kawir told Gecko that he could never be Iteung's lover. He could never be any woman's lover, because he would never be able to give them what they needed.

—

They were sitting on the patio with a plate of fried cassava that Wa Sami had made and warm *bajigur* that they'd bought from a passing vendor. Sipping on the sweet coconut milk, they were reminiscing about the distant past, wondering what had happened to all of their elementary school friends, when a figure appeared out in the darkness. A rain was starting to fall with gathering momentum, when the two boys realized the figure was running toward them. It was Iteung. The girl slowed before them, approaching Ajo Kawir. They looked at each other for a few moments. There was a reluctance in Ajo Kawir's eyes, maybe because he was still embarrassed about their last meeting and the fact that he'd never contacted the girl since. Iteung seemed nervous about what she was about to do and she was shivering, completely drenched. And then, she took Ajo Kawir's hand.

"I know you don't want to see me," she said, gathering her courage. Now she looked right into Ajo Kawir's eyes. "Where have you been? Why didn't you answer any of my songs on the radio? Why are you avoiding me?" At this point it seemed as though the girl began to cry, although it was hard to distinguish tears from the raindrops on her wet face. "Be my lover. I miss you so much. It's been torture waiting to hear from you. I want to kiss you, I want you to hold me, I want to make love to you. Be my lover." She was practically begging. She looked nothing like the girl who had fought against Ajo Kawir, the girl who couldn't be defeated.

Gecko saw the flash of fear in Ajo Kawir's eyes, but he was still flabbergasted when he saw him shake his head.

"What is it?" the girl asked.

"I can't. I can't be your lover. You are light and I'm pitch black darkness, something that you will never understand." Of course, he wanted to say something else, but his mouth wouldn't form the words: *I can't get an erection.*

The girl froze for a moment, looking at Ajo Kawir in disbelief. Then she let go of his hand. Her eyes welled up—now her tears were obvious, spilling down her cheeks.

"You're awful!"

The girl backed away off the terrace, into the storm. She stood there for a few moments, and then she turned and ran through the rain, leaving them behind.

Gecko was stunned by everything that had happened—all he could do was stare. Then he looked over at Ajo Kawir, who was also frozen in silence. Suddenly, he slapped his friend's face, dumbfounding him.

"You idiot! That girl loves you. Don't do something that you will regret. Go after her. Now!"

Gecko shoved Ajo Kawir out into the rain.

❊{ 3 }❊

SOME PEOPLE SAID that he went to Jakarta to get away from Iteung. Some said that he was trying to get away from the whole business with the Tiger. But he told Gecko before he left: "I won't come back until my dick can get hard."

Gecko would wait patiently, sincerely praying that Ajo Kawir's bird would be able to stand up once again. Like when they were still just barely teenagers, before that whole incident at Scarlet Blush's house.

—

But there he stood in the rain, silently staring toward the empty space where the girl had just been. The rainstorm was steadily picking up, but he just kept standing there. His clothes stuck to his body.

"Go after that girl, you idiot! You stupid, fucking idiot!"

But Ajo Kawir just kept standing there, staring off in the same direction. His skin began to turn pale. He started to shiver. He still didn't move.

Damn, thought Gecko, and he stopped yelling. He fell silent on the patio, looking out at his friend standing in the rain. He knew that the kid wouldn't last out there much longer, he was clearly freezing and might get sick. Unable to contain himself, Gecko jumped out into the deluge and dragged Ajo Kawir back onto the patio. Then he brought him inside, toward the kitchen.

Ajo Kawir wasn't just shivering—now his lips were blue. Gecko threw a towel over him.

"I'm sorry, I think I got a little carried away."

Of course Gecko had gotten carried away. Ajo Kawir had told him many times that there was no way that he could ever fall in love with a woman—it wasn't that he wasn't interested in women, but he had nothing to offer them. A man who cannot take a woman to bed, he would say in a tone so wise, so jaded, and so sorry for himself, is like a rusty blade that can't be used to cut anything. We shouldn't even be talking about it.

—

Gecko awoke early in the morning. Ajo Kawir wasn't sleeping next to him. Since he rarely slept at his own house, Ajo Kawir usually slept with Gecko in his room, or sometimes he slept in the back of the store. Sometimes he fell sleep at the security post not far from Iwan Angsa's house, but Gecko was certain that earlier that night, before he'd fallen asleep, Ajo Kawir had been in the bed. He turned on the light. He was alone.

Stumbling a bit, he went out of the bedroom. He heard the sound of a door being opened and closed. Maybe that's what had woken him up. Maybe it's Ajo Kawir, he thought. The sound had come from the store. There was a door in between the house and the shop. He went through it.

The store was dark, illuminated only by the dim glow from the refrigerator where they kept the cans and bottles of cold drinks, and he saw that the front door was slightly ajar.

"Ajo?"

He didn't hear the kid answer. Gecko opened the front door and found his friend sitting on the patio, an open bottle of Bintang beer beside him.

Sitting down in the empty chair next to Ajo Kawir, Gecko picked up the bottle of beer, took a few swigs, and placed it back down.

For some moments neither of them said anything. They took turns drinking beer from the bottle. After the beer was finished, Gecko finally spoke.

"You could die from this."

"What do you mean?"

"You haven't slept for days. And you haven't eaten anything, I know you haven't even had a bite."

Ajo Kawir didn't respond. He left Gecko and went inside the store, soon returning with a new bottle of beer. He opened the cap by pounding it against the edge of the table. The foam hissed.

"You're going to have to pay for these two bottles of beer. I don't want my mother saying I stole them in the middle of the night."

"Of course I'll pay for them."

After that, they both went back to daydreaming. They still took turns drinking the beer, but they didn't finish it as fast as they'd finished the first one. Gecko thought, you can't stop someone from falling in love. Not even the person who is falling in love can stop it. Love is like a sickness. It can strike at any time, like lightning or thunder, for no good reason. And even when there's a good reason for *not* falling in love, like Ajo Kawir has, love is something that simply cannot be avoided.

"You could die from it," Gecko said again. "You could die from not eating and not sleeping."

"I don't care."

"You won't be able to forget her."

Ajo Kawir didn't reply. He chugged the beer until it was fin-ished. He held the bottle and looked out into the darkness. There was a small road in front of the store, but nobody was going by at this hour. In the distance, someone struck the electricity pole three times. Usually it was the night guard who did that, a sign that all was safe and people could keep sleeping peacefully.

"I want to beat someone up."

"I don't think this is a good time to beat anyone up. There are no dumbass kids roaming about at this time of night."

———

"I've been looking for you everywhere, I thought you didn't want to go back to your house. My father sent me—you said you wanted to beat someone up? Well I have a good offer. My father said it would be better if you didn't accept it, and I don't think you should either. But I figured I had to tell you about it, and my father agreed. You can beat someone up, and you can earn some money doing it. But I still think you shouldn't."

———

The man came from Jakarta. He was wearing dark sunglasses when he first arrived, but then he took them off. He had on a Hawaiian shirt with the top two buttons unbuttoned. I swear to God, Ajo Kawir said to himself, I will *never* wear a shirt like that. He was wearing khaki-colored knee-length shorts and Adidas sneakers. He was with a driver who looked and acted like a bodyguard. "Call me Uncle Bunny."

"Okay, Uncle Bunny," Ajo Kawir mumbled.

Uncle Bunny felt around in his pocket and took out a box of

cigars. He offered one to Ajo Kawir. Ajo Kawir had never smoked cigars and had never wanted to. He shook his head. He pointed toward a pack of cloves on the table as if to say, I have cloves and that's all I want to smoke. But he didn't want to smoke a clove right then. He just wanted to hear whatever it was that Uncle Bunny had to say.

The man was about sixty years old, maybe older. He held the edge of his cigar to the flame of his lighter for a moment, until the edge was burnt and the tobacco leaves were crackling with sparks, and then Uncle Bunny smoked his cigar. Ajo Kawir liked the aroma it gave off.

"So you're the one who cut off Mister Lebe's ear?"

"How do you know about that?" Ajo Kawir asked, taken aback.

Uncle Bunny chuckled. He lit his cigar again and inhaled. "You may think that not many people would know about a thing like that, but certain information does reach my ears."

Ajo Kawir nodded.

"And now I want you to rough up another guy. He's older than you, a lot older. And maybe stronger. People call him the Tiger."

—

"The Tiger?" asked Iwan Angsa. Before he met with Ajo Kawir, Uncle Bunny had gone to see Iwan Angsa. "I know that guy. Or, I know about him but I don't know him. I fought his older brother once. It was an unforgettable fight … He was the most brutal man I ever met—meaning, his brother."

"He's more brutal than his brother."

"That's what I've heard."

"His brother is dead. Someone shot him in the street and threw him into a muddy rice paddy. It was around the same time they killed Agus Cornpipe, but they only found him three or four months later. The Tiger took over all his older brother's business. He's more brutal, more difficult to control, and he doesn't listen to anyone. He's fought with more people and killed more of them than his brother ever did. And he's never been caught. Or, he hasn't been caught yet."

"I'm grateful I don't have to fight him," said Iwan Angsa.

"You're afraid of a guy like that?"

"I'm not afraid of him," Iwan Angsa replied. "But not fighting him is way better for my chances of survival."

"I want you to kill him."

———

Iwan Angsa invited Uncle Bunny and his driver to eat at the house.

"It's just village food," he said, to be polite.

Uncle Bunny was happy with his hospitality. "Well, I'm a village guy," he replied.

"I've traveled to many places, and sometimes on your dime," said Iwan Angsa. "I've roamed here and there, gone exploring from one city to the next—Jakarta, Surabaya, Medan, Makassar. I almost died in Tanjung Priuk, I was attacked by a guy in the hull of a Pelni boat. But after all that I came back home to this little town, and started my life again."

"Because I saved you."

Yeah, Iwan Angsa knew that. He and Agus Cornpipe did something stupid when they robbed a general's nephew and gouged out his eyes. They were hunted everywhere. Put in prison, still a target. Uncle Bunny came and saved them—he knew the general well, and said that actually he didn't care that his nephew didn't have eyes anymore, and they got out of jail. And then Uncle Bunny told Iwan Angsa to kill a policeman who kept coming to his factory, before sending him off to roam around. And then Agus Cornpipe shot that woman who wanted Uncle Bunny to marry her.

"And I always protected you."

"Yeah, but after that I got married and I reformed. I don't want to fight anymore."

"I know you don't. But I need someone like you to stop the Tiger."

"I don't want the job," Iwan Angsa said. "I have a wife and kid to take care of."

"I know. I knew that when I came here, and I knew you'd refuse. I'm sorry about what happened all those years ago, and also about the death of your friend. But you know, politics is way scarier than your average street fight."

"You said it."

"What about your son? They say that he could do the kinds of things you used to do, if he wanted to."

"Gecko? For God's sake, I don't want him to follow in my foot-steps. He likes fighting, and sometimes he fights and I can't stop him. But I don't think he'd want the job. To a certain extent, I've been able to tame his instincts. He's been kicked out of school many times, but I hope that he'll continue with his education. I keep trying until I'm blue in the face to convince him to go to Yo-gyakarta or Bandung for college. He doesn't need to fight like his dad. And I'm pretty sure he won't want to fight for your money. I hope he won't fight for anybody's money."

"That's what I expected."

———

Uncle Bunny looked at Iwan Angsa for a long time. They had finished eating, but they hadn't moved from the dining table. Iwan

Angsa knew that Uncle Bunny wouldn't leave without finding someone to take care of his business with the Tiger.

"I hate to say this, but there is one kid who might be interested."

"Tell me."

"His name's Ajo Kawir. I look after him, everything that happens to him is my responsibility. I'd prefer that he didn't accept your offer, but, with or without your offer he'll be fighting with people—sooner or later he'll probably get killed. So maybe in the meantime there's some good if he can fight and at least earn some money."

"Sounds like an interesting kid."

"He might not actually need your money, but he would probably be happy to have an excuse to fight."

"That sounds great."

"But if he refuses, then our business stops there."

"Agreed. Where can I find him?"

"Gecko will take you."

Iwan Angsa thought about Ajo Kawir's dick.

———

Ajo Kawir finally took one of his cloves, lit it, and smoked it. He had never received an offer like this, and he was happy—his hands were shaking from excitement and he had to fight for self-control.

"All you need to do is eliminate the Tiger without a trace, as if he'd plunged into one of Krakatoa's craters and is never coming back. Do you know where Krakatoa is?"

"I'm not an idiot."

Uncle Bunny laughed. "If you can send him to the bottom of a Krakatoa crater, there's a lot of money in it for you."

"In other words, kill him."

"Yeah, kill him. Without letting on that there is any connection to me."

Ajo Kawir nodded. He took another drag on his cigarette, and exhaled the smoke. It gathered in a thick cloud around his face, curling around the strands of his hair.

"I'll duel him. A duel is a way to kill him without it ever being traced back to you. Your name will never come up, Uncle."

"You're smart, kid," said Uncle Bunny. "I'm happy to hear it."

"I'll take the job. But I want to see the money, General."

"You're kind of goofy, though, too, aren't you. Call me Uncle Bunny."

—

"You don't need to take this job," Gecko said.

"Yes, I do need this job," Ajo Kawir replied.

"No, you don't need it. You don't need any money. You're always saving your money because you don't even know what to do with it. You don't need to kill the Tiger."

"I do need this job. I need to do something to forget that girl. I want to forget Iteung, forget love. I *need* to fight. And now someone wants to pay me to fight."

—

The Tiger was not the kind of person who was easy to find. He roamed around. His house was in Ci Jaro, but he was only there about one or two days out of the year. More often, he was at large.

"I don't care how you find him, or how you kill him, as long as my name isn't involved. I can't give you any more guidance than this old photograph, just so you don't attack the wrong guy."

Uncle Bunny gave him a photo. It was a color photo but in a number of spots the color was already peeling off, faded to sepia. In the photo there were three men sitting on a big rock showing off a pig. They had clearly just been hunting and the pig was either dying or already dead. The man on the left had been circled with a ballpoint pen. Ajo Kawir didn't have to ask—of course that man was the Tiger.

"You don't need to know what he did, and you don't need to know what my business is with him," said Uncle Bunny.

"I don't even care," replied Ajo Kawir. "I just need your money, and above all, I need someone to fight me."

"Good."

—

Iwan Angsa had given him advice, time and again, about how fighting was the worst way to make a living. But clearly Ajo Kawir hadn't listened, especially once his pecker stopped standing up. He got into fights almost every week. He went to the movie theater, not to watch a movie but to look for other kids to provoke into boxing him in the street. He went to the swimming pool not to look at the pretty girls in their bikinis, but to fight in the water. He went to the dingdong parlor not to play the slots but to play on the nerves of the other patrons.

"This kid is going to turn into the most terrifying fighter I've ever known," Iwan Angsa muttered to his wife.

"He'll only stop once his dick can stand up again," Wa Sami replied.

"It's true. But I don't know whether it ever will."

"That poor kid."

—

Ajo Kawir's father was a respectable person, a government employee who worked in the local library. But what with all of Ajo

Kawir's behavior, he had finally given up. One day he sought out Iwan Angsa and told him, "I don't know what else to do. He never listens to me when I talk to him."

"As far as I can tell, he only reacts when he hears a fart," replied Iwan Angsa.

And ever since then, Iwan Angsa was the only person keeping track of him. Iwan Angsa knew when he fought, and with whom. And his wife, Wa Sami, was the one who bandaged the kid up whenever he came home all black and blue. After a while, because of his friendship with Gecko, Ajo Kawir more or less stayed at their house. He helped watch the store, or helped haul goods. When that was done, he'd go out in the afternoon or the evening, hoping to get in some punches.

Iwan Angsa finally said, "At least fight for money. I don't want you to die for nothing."

And that's why Iwan Angsa was ready to pass the offer of killing the Tiger on to Ajo Kawir.

And when Wa Sami heard that Ajo Kawir took the offer, she quietly mumbled, "I'm worried that this time, you won't need me to wrap your wounds and bruises, you'll need me to sprinkle you with Borax and wrap you in a burial shroud."

Iwan Angsa said, "I'm more afraid that one day, they won't be able to contain these scoundrels anymore, and they'll decide to kill them off, one by one. Like how they killed Agus Cornpipe. Like how they killed the Tiger's older brother."

—

"Even though I'm not sure he's there, there's no other choice but to go to Ci Jaro to find the Tiger," Iwan Angsa said. Uncle Bunny agreed, Gecko thought the same thing, and Ajo Kawir thought so too. "One or two of his family members must live there, or there will be somebody who knows him."

At first, Ajo Kawir was going to go alone, but Iwan Angsa had told Gecko to go with him. "Don't be stupid," Iwan Angsa said. "Ci Jaro's a settlement of robbers and thieves. If they don't like the looks of you, they'll swindle or ambush you." So the next morning, with Gecko at his side, Ajo Kawir headed out for Ci Jaro, a small village two hours away.

The boys arrived there near midday. There were only about a dozen houses in the village. In the center of town, some *ojek* motorcycle drivers for hire were hanging out next to a couple of small food stalls by the side of the road. Other people stopped by briefly, just to drink some coffee or eat some fried snacks.

Gecko had slipped a knife into his jeans. He hoped he wouldn't have to use it, but if anything happened, he wouldn't run. He wouldn't abandon Ajo Kawir. He knew they were going to an unfamiliar place, and were looking for an enemy who had power there. Something bad could happen. But he tried to stay calm. There were always policemen around. And soldiers. If there was some commotion, then there would be some commotion, and nothing more than that. He really hoped he wouldn't need to take the knife out.

—

They sat on a bench at one of the food stalls and ordered two glasses of black coffee, no sugar. They asked for rice, *sayur lodeh*—vegetables cooked in coconut milk—and fried catfish, and they both took some fried tempeh and a spoonful of fermented shrimp paste. They were starving. They didn't want to start their business hungry. They both ate ravenously, without saying a word.

The food stall owner was an old woman. She was busy with her stove, frying tempeh and tofu. She would fan the flame with a piece of woven bamboo whenever she thought it was dying down and stoke it with a couple of pieces of wood or dried coconut rinds to keep the fire going.

Every once in a while she looked over at the two boys sitting on the bench eating. She'd never seen them before. She was probably wondering what business had brought these two strange kids to her *warung*, and to her village.

Meanwhile two *ojek* drivers, about their age, were sitting on their worn out Honda motorbikes, watching Ajo Kawir and Gecko. They appeared to be talking to each other but so low that it was hard to tell. Ajo Kawir didn't care. And Gecko didn't care either. They were hungry. All they wanted to do right then was eat.

—

"You know, the worst thing that you could do is not kill the Tiger, but let *him* kill *you*. Or even worse than that would be if it wasn't the Tiger who killed you, but just someone else who wasn't happy to hear that you want to kill him."

"If I die," said Ajo Kawir, "then my business with that girl is over. I will forget Iteung forever. And I won't have to suffer anymore because my pecker can't stand up."

"I don't want you to die."

"I don't want to die either. So, I won't."

—

After they had finished eating and had their coffee, Ajo Kawir finally said, "I'm looking for the Tiger. I know he's from Ci Jaro. Where can I find him?"

He asked the old woman who owned the food stall, but he spoke loudly enough so that the two *ojek* drivers would hear him too. He didn't glance at them, though, pretending he hadn't even noticed they were there, and looked straight at the old woman.

"He hasn't come back here ever since his older brother died."

"Don't exaggerate," Ajo Kawir replied in a condescending tone. "He's been back a couple of times. Not often, but he's been here."

The old woman didn't seem to like Ajo Kawir talking back. She turned away, fanned the fire in her stove, and then turned again, looking at the two kids, maybe trying to guess how old they were.

"How can I find him?"

"I don't know," the old woman said. She sounded a bit cross. "If I knew, I would already have gone to find him myself. He's racked up some debts at my stall and I want him to pay me before I die."

"I know he's not here now," Ajo Kawir said. "But if he shows up, or if someone sees him, tell him that someone is looking for him, that there's someone who wants to challenge him to a duel. I want to fight him. It's up to the Tiger when and where—whatever he says, I'll accept. And after that, I don't mind squaring all of the Tiger's debts with you here."

After he said that, silence descended. There was nothing but the crackling of the fire burning the dried coconut fronds in the stove. The woman was quiet, looking at the two kids, before she went back to her stove and flipped the tempeh in her frying pan. The two *ojek* drivers were silent too, exchanging glances. Ajo Kawir reached for a pack of cloves that was sitting on top of a jar, took out one cigarette, and lit it with the lighter that was hanging from a string above the tray of fried snacks.

Gecko finally broke the silence by asking how much they owed. He paid with some money from his pocket, checking that the knife was still there. They were getting ready to leave when the *warung* owner asked them:

"So what's your business with the Tiger?"

"An old grudge. If I don't take care of it now, then it will last for seven generations."

Iwan Angsa had told Ajo Kawir to say that, and he did. Actually, Iwan Angsa had also told him to look for the Tiger in secret, but Ajo Kawir decided to challenge him to a duel outright. He figured that was the only way that people wouldn't think he was doing it for Uncle Bunny.

After eating at the *warung* in Ci Jaro, the two boys headed for home. They walked to where the bus would pass by, which wasn't too far from the food stall, only about fifty meters, but before they got there, they heard the sound of two motorbikes approaching.

The two *ojek* swept by, suddenly turned, and braked, making a barricade right in front of Ajo Kawir and Gecko, who stopped walking and glowered at them. The two drivers glowered right back.

We are going to fight right here in the road, thought Gecko.

"Who are you two?" one of the drivers asked.

Neither Ajo Kawir nor Gecko replied, they just stood there glaring at the two drivers. They didn't want any small talk—if they were going to fight, better to just get to it.

"Who are you, so that the Tiger can know who to look for and reply to your challenge?"

"Ajo Kawir," Ajo Kawir finally said. "Tell him, Ajo Kawir from Bojong Soang is challenging him to a duel. Everyone in Bojong Soang knows me."

"You'll have to wait," said the other driver. "I don't know for how long, but you'll have to wait."

After saying that, he drove off and his friend followed. They went back to the *warung*, and parked. Ajo Kawir and Gecko watched them for a few more moments, but then they heard the bus rumbling in the distance and they hurried on.

—

In the early morning, even before the sun appeared, he'd leave Wa Sami's store and put on the fake Nikes that he'd bought in the market. He'd run along the main street toward the center of the city, circling the large mosque toward the stadium before heading back. Sometimes Gecko would come with him, but more often he told him to go running alone, preferring to sleep in.

"It's way more important for you not to fight than it is for you to stay in perfect shape," Gecko said.

"I know."

"Don't fight and get beat up. We never know when the Tiger is going to appear."

"That's what I hate about it. I hate that I don't know when he's going to show."

"Well, the smart thing for you to do, at least, would be to not fight in the meantime. Because if you fight, there's always the possibility you'll get beat up or injured. You have to keep yourself strong. You don't know how hard it's going to be to defeat the Tiger, and you have to do more than that—you have to kill him."

"Shut up, I don't want this kind of advice."

—

He waited. He hated waiting, but he had no choice. The good part was that he started eating ravenously, like a nineteen-year-old kid should. Iwan Angsa was happy to see him eat so much. Whatever happened, the boy wasn't even twenty yet, but Iwan Angsa hated to think about that. He hated to think that a kid that age would have to fight the Tiger, and he especially hated to think about what might become his fate. But he was happy to see him stuff his face.

"I think that now I'm going to die from boredom. I'm sick of waiting," Ajo Kawir said crankily.

Maybe because he was bored with waiting, he found himself thinking about Iteung even more. Sometimes he remembered their fight, other times he remembered the brush of her lips. Sometimes he remembered what it felt like when he caressed her breasts, and how it felt when he had stuck his middle finger between her legs.

"It's like I can still feel her breasts in the palms of my hands," Ajo Kawir said.

"I don't know what you're talking about. I've never touched a woman's boobs."

"Maybe I won't die from fighting after all," he continued to Gecko, in a tragic tone. "Maybe I'll die from boredom, but most likely of all, I'll die from this suffocating longing."

There was nothing Gecko could do.

—

Of course, what Gecko really wanted to say was, just go see that girl right away, you idiot. Maybe Iteung already forgot all about you, maybe she doesn't love you anymore, maybe she found a new guy, maybe she thinks you're a piece of shit, maybe she thinks you're a pathetic loser, but it will still be way better to see her than not to. Tell her you love her and that you regret rejecting her love.

But all that just hummed inside Gecko's head. He could have said it, but he didn't want to mention anything that had to do with Ajo Kawir's privates. Iteung didn't just need love, she needed someone who could take her to bed.

"I'm in the mood for a fight."

"Wait for the Tiger to show up."

—

If there were any days that were the most depressing in the life of Ajo Kawir, it could be said that those were the days. When the store was closed, he'd lock himself inside alone, drinking beers and crying. Gecko knew that Ajo Kawir was crying—even men need to cry sometimes—but Gecko wasn't sure what exactly was making Ajo Kawir cry. Maybe he was crying because his dick couldn't stand up (he had cried about that before, Gecko had seen him); maybe it was because he longed for Iteung (and it really is quite sad when you can't have what you know should be yours); or maybe it was actually because he was scared of coming face to face with the Tiger (because, in fact, Ajo Kawir had never killed anyone, but it was well known that the Tiger himself had killed more than a few).

Even Gecko got the shivers imagining Ajo Kawir killing someone.

—

After Ajo Kawir had been in that sorry state for a while, with no indication that the Tiger was going to appear, Gecko finally found him in a corner of the store, slumped behind a pile of sacks filled with rice.

"Come on, let's go find Iteung."

Ajo Kawir didn't seem at all interested.

"You won't have to greet her, or even talk to her. We can just go look at her from a distance. I'm sure that it will heal those gaping wounds in your heart, just a little bit." As he said that, Gecko pointed at Ajo Kawir's chest, or more exactly, nudged it with his index finger. In his weak despondency, Ajo Kawir's torso swayed backward from that gentle push. He still wasn't at all interested in the idea. Or more precisely, he pretended he wasn't interested.

—

Gecko was taking a nap in his room when Ajo Kawir came in and woke him up. Annoyed, Gecko turned around to glare at him. He hadn't slept at all the night before, had just fallen asleep less than a half an hour ago, and wanted to be left alone. But Ajo Kawir didn't care. He stood next to Gecko's bed, looking down at his friend with a pitiful face.

"I want to go see Iteung," he said.

That was enough to erase all of Gecko's annoyance. He sat up in bed, and looked at his friend.

Ajo Kawir admitted that all this time he had been carrying Iteung's photo around in his wallet, looking at it every night before he fell asleep, and now he wanted to see her in real life. He wanted to see her walk, see her smile—he even wanted to see her fight. Ajo Kawir showed Gecko the photo. It was already starting to fade, maybe because it had been taken out of its spot so often.

"But I'm afraid to see her, more afraid than of meeting all of my enemies at once."

"You don't have to be afraid," replied Gecko. "If she spots you following her and she gets mad at you and attacks you, well, there's nothing more beautiful in this world than dying in the arms of someone you love."

Actually, Gecko was just saying that for show. He didn't really know anything about love. He himself had been rejected twice, by two different girls, and had never had a steady girlfriend. Maybe he had heard the phrase somewhere, in a song lyric or a cowboy movie—he thought that it would sound good if he could talk about love and death, so he said it just to say it, not really to be helpful, but it was because he had said it that Ajo Kawir finally had the nerve to go find Iteung.

"I'll see her. Maybe it wouldn't be so bad if she attacks me and kills me. And if not, and then later I'm killed by the Tiger, well at least I will have seen her again."

—

When he finally saw her, one kick from that girl made him fall, or more exactly hurled him down into the grass. He lay there, with an excruciating pain in his chest. But he tried to smile and, with great difficulty, tried to get up again. His body wasn't fully upright, both his legs still felt shaky, when the girl gave him another kick, right in his crotch. He grimaced, but his mouth was swollen from one of the girl's right hooks and his lip had split—he tasted his own sweet blood.

"Why aren't you doing anything?!" the girl demanded. "Come on, fight back!"

Ajo Kawir tried to smile. His lip hurt, but he smiled. His eyes, gazing on Iteung, were shining. He was happy to see her hair that rippled out when she lunged at him, pummeled him. He was happy to see her face, which was turning red as she held back her rage. He was happy to see her fiery eyes, exuding hatred.

"Say something, you shit!"

Ajo Kawir couldn't say anything. All he could do was smile. A little grin.

—

Gecko took him to go see Iteung. They went to the martial arts academy where she had said she practiced. They didn't go inside, they just waited across the street, sitting on a bench belonging to a *cendol* seller. They drank two glasses of shaved ice each, but they still didn't see Iteung. All they saw were small children in their school uniforms going into the building and a couple of teenage girls coming out, ready to go home. They had taken their uniforms off, and now they were wearing their exercise clothes.

"Maybe we need to go in there and ask them," Gecko said, feeling bored.

"I don't want Iteung to know I am looking for her."

So they kept waiting, until midday turned into afternoon. A few more people came out of the academy, but Iteung was not among them. It seemed clear that she hadn't gone there that day. Or maybe she was no longer going there at all—she'd only said she had studied there, not that she was still studying there.

Without a word, Ajo Kawir stood up and gave the *cendol* seller some money, and then set off along the sidewalk. He walked off just like that, as if he had forgotten that he was there with Gecko. Gecko stood up and chased after him, half running.

"Where are you going?"

"Home."

—

The blows struck his face again and again. He had never endured such fast-paced punches. Her right and left fists took turns pummeling his cheeks, forehead, and chin. At first he just let the blows fall where they would. But after a while they began to really sting. His forehead was cut. He tried to dodge, but the attack was inescapable. He felt his cheek swelling. His eyelids seemed to grow smaller and tighter, maybe they were swollen too. Until finally, one unavoidable punch sent him off, floating. The last thing he remembered was something slamming against his back. Oh, no, it wasn't that—it was his back, slamming against the ground.

—

"We could go to her house if you want. You know where she lives, and what would make the most sense, if you want to see her, would be to go to her house."

"I ..."

"What? Are you going to say you are too scared to see her? You said you wanted to die in her arms. If that's what you want, then we can go to her house, knock on her door, and see what she'll do to you—what she'll do to the man who let her run off crying in the rain."

"Don't talk about that ever again."

"She ran off into the rain, crying."

"Stop."

"She ran off into the rain, crying."

"You monkey. Forget it. I don't want to see her anymore."

—

He thought he lost consciousness after slamming onto the ground, or if he didn't lose consciousness, he lost track of how long he had been lying there. He opened his eyes. His whole body felt shattered to pieces. He looked up at the sky, and it looked unusual. He blinked—it looked so low, so close. He blinked a few more times, weak blinks, and then tried to get up, but his body felt too heavy.

"Go ahead," he heard the girl say. "I thought you couldn't get up."

"I will get up as long as I can get up," Ajo Kawir said, trying to smile.

"All right, then I guess I will have to make it so that you'll never get up ever again."

—

Ajo Kawir was just wearing shorts, with no shirt. His chiseled torso was covered in scars. A towel was slung over his shoulder. He was sitting on a big rock next to the house, at a spring where the neighbors did their laundry. He liked bathing there, drawing the water from the spring and then pouring it over his body. But that afternoon he hadn't bathed yet. He was just sitting on that big rock, kept company by a bottle of beer that he had taken from the refrigerator in Wa Sami's corner store.

"What are you doing?" Gecko asked when he found him daydreaming on top of that rock.

"I'm waiting for the Tiger."

"Maybe he's scared of you. Maybe he'll never come because he's scared of you. Or if he does show up, maybe it'll be two years from now—or twelve years, or twenty years from now. Forget about the Tiger. You don't really need the money all that much."

Ajo Kawir's face displayed a kind of vexation and all of a sudden he slammed the bottle of beer down against the rock. It broke into smithereens. Gecko had to jump out of the way of the pieces of shattered glass that went flying. Ajo Kawir was lucky that none of them cut his leg.

"You're a jerk!" Gecko yelled. "The beer is sold separately from the bottle. You're going to have to pay for that bottle."

"I don't give a shit. I'll pay for it."

After saying that, he threw what was left of the bottle, the jagged neck that he was still holding, toward the banana orchard.

"Tomorrow I'm going to see Iteung."

—

His legs still felt unsteady, but the girl gave him another punch and once again he was sent reeling backward into the grass—grass with hard dirt underneath it. He felt like he could no longer move at all. He was finished. He didn't regret it. He was happy. He was happy to feel the girl's punches all over his body. He was happy to feel her so close to him.

Iteung approached. She lifted up Ajo Kawir's left foot, and then placed her foot on his knee.

She could break my leg with one quick stamp, Ajo Kawir thought. Or at least, she could break his kneecap, or dislocate it. He didn't care. He was willing to have his leg broken, as long as it was Iteung who was breaking it. He waited for a loud *craaack* to come from his left leg. He didn't want to close his eyes. He looked at the girl, hoping to watch her do it.

"I could break your leg right now," Iteung said, "but I don't feel like it." She released her grip on Ajo Kawir's left leg, and it fell back onto the ground. "But I would be happy to give you a bloody nose."

As soon as those words were out of her mouth, the ultimate punch came, and that one really made his nose spout—blood immediately poured out of his nostrils, and Ajo Kawir felt his spirit fly, to who knows where.

His vision blurred. The sky drew even closer. He looked over. The girl shook the blood off her hand. Then she walked away and was nothing but a silhouette.

"Iteung," he stammered. He didn't know whether the girl heard him or not. He almost couldn't even hear his own voice. "I … I love you."

He saw the shadow of the girl stop in her tracks, and then he couldn't see anything anymore.

—

They were standing before the house's front door, knocking on it. A middle-aged woman opened it. Ajo Kawir introduced himself and said he would like to see Iteung. The woman looked at him for a long time and then suddenly she smiled.

"Oh, so this is Ajo Kawir," she murmured. "Iteung talks about you all the time. I think she has been sad that she couldn't see you. I don't know what happened between you two, she never tells me anything. She just calls out your name in her sleep. I don't know whether you two are dating or not, but she calls your name all the time. She has been so sad."

"Can I see her?"

The woman smiled. "She's not here. If you don't want to wait, you can find her at Mister Lebe's fishpond. I don't know why she likes it there, but she has asked her father to take her there a number of times, and then all she does is sit there in the grass."

"I'll go to her there," said Ajo Kawir to Gecko. "Alone. You don't have to come."

—

"I'll say it once more, I can't get hard."

"I don't care, I still love you."

Not far from Mister Lebe's fishpond, Ajo Kawir was lying with his head resting in Iteung's lap. She bent down to hold him tight. She wiped the blood from the kid's nose. She caressed his face. Ajo Kawir reached up to return the caress, wiping the tears from Iteung's cheeks. Again and again, Iteung lifted Ajo Kawir's head and kissed it.

"What are you going to do with a guy who can't get hard?"

"I'm going to marry him."

❊{ 4 }❊

YEARS LATER, WHEN he met Jelita, Ajo Kawir often remembered that day—the day he decided to marry Iteung. In retrospect, he often felt that his decision was foolish, the most foolish thing he had ever done in his life. But who can stand in the way of love? He loved Iteung, and Iteung loved him. They both wanted to get married. They didn't care that the marriage would include a penis that couldn't stand up.

"After all, there are only five requirements for marriage, at least that's what I remember hearing in a sermon broadcast from the mosque," said Gecko. "One, there is a bride and groom. Two, there is someone to represent the woman. Three, there is a headman to marry them. Four, there's the marriage contract. Five, there is a witness." And what he said seemed to make sense.

—

Ajo Kawir needed about three weeks to recover from his injuries, and during that time, Gecko was terribly worried. He was worried that it would be exactly at a time like this that the Tiger would appear and respond to Ajo Kawir's challenge—the duel between them wasn't just a boxing match, which could be postponed if one of them wasn't ready, with money back on the purchased tickets.

"Don't worry," said Ajo Kawir. "Now I have a fiancée who can protect me from even the most brutal killer."

And he wasn't exaggerating. Gecko had never seen Iteung fight, but he'd heard Ajo Kawir's story about their first brawl, and now he saw for himself his friend's fresh wounds. With Iteung by his side, Ajo Kawir really didn't have anything to worry about.

—

"One day the Tiger had a toothache, but he didn't want to go to the dentist. He never went to the dentist, just like he never went to the barber for a shave. He always thought that they could kill him too easily, just like someone had killed his older brother. It was true that the recent rash of mysterious killings had stopped, but he was still afraid. He didn't want to be lying there, trapped in the chair, and have the dentist drill his eyes out, or rip them out with a pair of pliers, or have the barber slit his throat with a razor. So he howled the whole night long with his toothache and no one dared approach him," said Iteung.

She was recounting this while sitting in a pedicab with Ajo Kawir beside her, holding her hand and resting his head on her shoulder. They were on their way back from watching a film at the movie theater.

"Where'd you hear that story?"

"I heard it," said Iteung. "The Empty Hand has many ears and mouths. They hear things from everywhere—and their mouths are as loose and full of chatter as a babbling baby."

"Do they know where the Tiger is?"

"I'm not sure. That's maybe the one thing they haven't heard.

Some people say he's in Jakarta, but others say that he's in Thailand, or maybe Macau. No one's really certain."

"And what about his toothache?" asked Ajo Kawir, intrigued.

"He cut off his left pinkie finger, so that he'd be distracted by a worse pain—that's what the Tiger is like. I don't know if that story's true or not, but that's what the Tiger is like. Anyone who's ever seen him will swear that he doesn't have a left pinkie, and it's because of that toothache. He's ruthless, even toward himself."

"He'll meet me," said Ajo Kawir. "And I'll put an end to his ruthlessness."

—

"Darling, you don't have to fight the Tiger. You have no real business with him."

Ajo Kawir thought about that. He had accepted the offer to fight the Tiger—to kill him—because he'd wanted to forget about his love for Iteung. But now he didn't want to forget it. He didn't want to forget Iteung at all, now that he had her.

"If I can kill him, I'll make a lot of money. I can use that money to marry you."

"We don't need a lot of money to get married. We could get married right now with the money in your wallet."

—

The Tiger yanked him by his hair, shoving him down into the water. He tried to fight back, but the Tiger was way too strong. He held his breath and opened his eyes wide, but all he could see was murky brown rays of light—the cloudy water of the Cidaho River. His chest felt like it was going to explode. His lungs begged him to open his mouth. But his two lips were clamped shut. His cheeks puffed out. His chest got even tighter. His eyes opened even wider. At first he could see the muddy Cidaho, but after a while all he could see was a blinding white light. He was dying.

The Tiger pulled him up to the surface and Ajo Kawir opened his mouth wide, gasping. Air and Cidaho water filled his lungs.

But when he tried to breathe in more air, the Tiger plunged him back down underwater. He thrashed about to get free. His arms flailed back and forth, his legs kicked. But the Tiger's grip was too strong. He felt like his lungs had already burst. Then whatever had been strangling his neck began to slowly disappear. His eyelids began to close.

Once again he was pulled to the surface. Once again he gasped for breath, his mouth gaping.

The Tiger let him go. He backed away slowly, his chest heaving, his mouth sputtering water and his eyes glazed over. His knees felt weak, his hands were trembling. He looked at the Tiger. Ajo Kawir wanted to raise his arms, to clench his hands, but all he could do was make weak fists.

Then a punch struck him squarely on the jaw. He felt himself flying, floating, and then landing on the surface of the water. His feet searched for the riverbed, but he couldn't find solid ground. He sank deeper.

—

Ajo Kawir awoke, gasping for air. His temples were drenched in sweat. Gecko woke up too, and looked over at him.

"What's wrong? A bad dream?"

"I'm afraid," said Ajo Kawir in a barely audible voice. "I'm afraid of the Tiger."

Gecko looked at him for a few minutes, as Ajo Kawir tried to calm himself down.

"I don't think you really need to fight him. Just forget about that money."

———

Iteung brought him to the martial arts academy, and after asking for permission from her teacher, they used the practice space in the middle of the night, when no other students were using it.

"With proper fighting technique and your brash recklessness, I'm sure no one will be able to defeat you."

"But I'm afraid I've already lost all my daring—I'm still worried the Tiger will defeat me."

"You can rescind your challenge, and return the advance money that you took from Uncle Bunny."

In fact, he had already considered that. Iteung was right, he didn't need to fight the Tiger. He was standing at the gate of happiness. He had found love. He was planning to marry his beloved. They would have a happy life together, even if it was a life without a dick that could stand up. He didn't need to risk all that for one pointless fight.

———

"But I'm a man," Ajo Kawir said to Gecko. "There's no way I can pull out once I've challenged someone to fight."

Gecko didn't say anything. He understood the dilemma. He knew Ajo Kawir was happy now, and he knew that his friend didn't want to get involved in anything that would deprive him of such happiness. But on the other hand, he had already run his mouth off in the Tiger's hometown, talking big and challenging him to a duel.

"Whatever happens, I'm a man. But I'm a man with a soft dick, so maybe I should just withdraw my challenge and run from the fight that I started myself. What a total loser."

Gecko hadn't seen Ajo Kawir cry in a long time, but now he saw his friend's eyes well up once more. He went to the shop and returned with an already-opened bottle of beer, and held it out to Ajo Kawir.

"Beer is every sad man's best friend. Drink it."

—

Iteung's parents were quite fond of Ajo Kawir. They invited him to come over every day, even if just for a quick lunch with them. They treated him like their own son, the son they never had—both of their children were girls. Ajo Kawir happily received their hospitality and accepted their frequent invitations.

Sometimes he helped fix a leak in their roof or a jammed water pump. Some days he took his future mother-in-law to the market, and other days he helped his future father-in-law paint the fence to welcome in Eid.

"I'm happy that you've helped our daughter become a woman again," his mother-in-law said. "I was often sad, watching her fight. She fought all the time. She climbed trees, went speeding around on her motorbike, hiking up mountains. Then she entered the martial arts academy and fought even more. But look at her now! Everywhere she goes, she wears a skirt. And this morning I saw her putting on lipstick."

Ajo Kawir smiled to hear this.

"She's really fallen in love with you."

And I've truly fallen in love with her.

—

"Mama wants us to get married as soon as possible," Iteung said. They were gazing into each other's eyes, the tips of their noses almost touching. "Do you want to marry me?"

"Of course. We've talked about it a lot already."

"But we're not even twenty years old yet."

"Who cares about that, I want to get married."

"Me too. I don't want to miss my chance to be happy with you."

Ajo Kawir was still looking at Iteung, their noses were still practically touching. Iteung smiled widely and Ajo Kawir returned her smile before asking, a bit uncertainly:

"But how can I make you happy?"

"I'm sure you will make me happy. I believe it. I know you can make me happy."

—

As soon as her parents left, Iteung closed the door and locked it, and then turned and stood, leaning against the door, looking at Ajo Kawir with an enticing smile. "Mama and Papa went to visit a distant neighbor celebrating their son's circumcision; they won't be back for at least two hours," she said, and smiled again, even more suggestively. "And my little sister won't be back for two hours either, because she's at a tutoring session." This time it was Ajo Kawir who smiled and approached her.

Before locking the door, Iteung had already closed the curtain so the room was cloaked in shadows. But they could still see each other, admire the shape of each other's faces.

Ajo Kawir drew closer and stood right in front of Iteung, placing both his hands around her waist. Iteung stood on her tiptoes, and crossed her arms behind Ajo Kawir's neck. Iteung began to smile, but Ajo Kawir stopped that smile with a kiss, and then another, and then another. Her lipstick tasted a little bit sweet, and slowly it grew wet and began to rub off, until all that was left was the natural color of her lips.

As they kissed, with their tongues slipping about and the occasional little nibble, Iteung pulled Ajo Kawir closer. Their bodies pressed tightly together and Ajo Kawir could feel the firm swell of her breasts. He gripped her hips, and Iteung clutched at his shoulders. The rhythm of their breathing grew urgent. Ajo Kawir stopped kissing her lips and began kissing her neck, the soft part under her ear. The girl looked up at him, and then her eyes closed.

Oh, thought Ajo Kawir, *if only my dick would stand up*.

—

Ajo Kawir had just realized that fingers were one of the most amazing blessings God granted to mankind. He often sat in front of Wa Sami's grocery store, looking down at his own ten fingers. "Think about it, "he said to Gecko. "How many animals can do what humans can do with their fingers?"

"Monkeys can grasp tree leaves with their toes," said Gecko.

"That's true," said Ajo Kawir, "I've seen them do it. But I think that only human fingers can fold paper, hold a pencil and write, pull a bow and arrow, hold a knife, and above all, make a woman happy."

"What do you mean?"

Ajo Kawir remembered how he had gently pushed Iteung onto the sofa and laid her down there. The fingers of one hand undid the buttons of her shirt while the fingers of the other hand still held her close. The five fingers of his right hand, in a way that he himself felt was astonishing, were able to unbutton her shirt, button by button. He had never known that buttons could be undone with just one hand, but that afternoon he did it. He opened her shirt and admired her body, which gently swelled with each breath she took.

"I actually think that human fingers have a mind of their own—they can do certain things without us even teaching them how."

"What do you mean?"

He had touched Iteung's breasts before. But that afternoon he didn't just touch them—he truly worshipped them. He could see his fingers slowly exploring them. If the girl's breasts were like a pair of small mountains, his fingers were like five hikers in no hurry to reach the summit. They took the scenic route, going up and down and around and around, as if they wanted to explore every section of the hill from every angle, without missing a thing. He watched his fingertips first go searching, then turn, letting the backs of his fingers and the smooth surface of his fingernails caress the soft skin of her breasts.

"With their fingers, people can feel something, express something. Sometimes their touch is like a message that can't be spoken in words."

"How long have you been thinking about this?"

Ajo Kawir just smiled. What human fingers can do is actually even more than that, he thought. My fingers, he thought, don't just explore her body. They can also give my woman pleasure. They can make my woman float. And that can be done with even only one finger, my index or middle finger, depending on which one I feel like using. I've done that before, but on that sofa, my woman showed my fingers how to do it better. I made her even happier than before. My fingers can do that for years, and maybe for many years in the future they will still be able to do what my dick can't do. My fingers are always extended and firm, even though they can't get any bigger. My fingers will never fall asleep.

"What is making you smile like that?" asked Gecko.

"I'm thinking about something that makes me happy."

"What?"

"We have already decided on a date for our wedding. I'm going to be happy. She is going to be happy. I'm going to turn twenty as a happy man."

Gecko nodded. He was happy to see the joy on Ajo Kawir's face. He patted his friend's shoulder and said:

"I think you're right, what you are saying about human fingers. We can use them to pick our noses—I've even seen people pick their noses with their thumbs, but I've never seen a chicken do it, or a goat, or a horse. Human fingers are truly amazing."

—

They had just gotten home from delivering some coconut oil to a family that owned a shrimp-chip factory when Wa Sami stopped them in front of her shop. She hesitated for a moment, but finally opened her mouth.

"Some kid is looking for you," she said to Ajo Kawir.

"Who?"

"I don't know. He just said he was looking for you. He seemed mad, but who isn't mad at the both of you for the way you act? He said he'd challenge you to a fight. He's going to stop you. He's going to make sure that your wedding to Iteung never happens. He said that he'd give you the most miserable day of your entire life."

"This kid ... Did he say the Tiger sent him?"

—

Two days later the phone in Wa Sami's store rang. Someone was looking for Ajo Kawir, and he was there to pick up, but whoever was on the other end only wanted to swear and curse at him.

"Who are you, asshole?" Ajo Kawir demanded.

"I'm the person who's going to fill your days with misery. Who's going to make sure that your wedding to that girl is nothing more than a dream that will never come true."

"Don't get my woman involved in this. If you want to fight, just tell me when and where."

"Oh, you'll meet me soon enough. Just pray that the day I come for you won't be the last day of your life."

"You asshole. I don't want to fight you. I want to fight the Tiger. Tell him to show himself, he doesn't need to send some snot-nosed kid like you in his place."

Laughing, the voice said, "Just pray, my friend. Pray it's not your day to die."

Then he hung up. Ajo Kawir slammed the phone down, fuming. Holding back his rage, he thought about Iteung. Why would the Tiger get her involved in this, he wondered. Maybe the Tiger knew that love was his one weakness. He was afraid to lose Iteung, afraid to lose his love. The Tiger would attack him at the moment he was at his weakest. He was furious, but at the same time his entire body shivered with terror.

—

Ajo Kawir walked along the side of the street. A car accosted him with its loud horn, accusing him of hogging the road. Startled, Ajo Kawir looked over and stood directly in front of the car, which was forced to slow to a stop right at the tips of his toes. He walked around toward the driver's side and ordered him to open up. With an idiotic expression, the man opened the door and Ajo Kawir immediately grabbed him, yanking him out of the vehicle. He didn't say anything, he just let his fists fly at the man's jaw. Once, twice, three times. He pushed the driver against the car and kept on assailing him. The driver tried to fend off the attack, but Ajo Kawir was too fast and fierce. Inside the car, a girl was screaming, but her screams didn't stop Ajo Kawir. Covered with blood, the driver had no chance to defend himself. Cars and motorcycles began to stop, and they tried to call Ajo Kawir off, but he'd already had enough. He walked away, leaving the driver sprawled out in the road, groaning next to the front wheels of his car.

—

"I have to finish this business with the Tiger before my wedding day," Ajo Kawir said.

Iteung was helping him bandage his right hand, which was swollen and smeared with blood after his impulsive attack.

"He sent that kid to threaten me and I can't just let that happen. I won't let him intimidate me. I won't let myself give in to fear. I'm going to stop him, before my wedding day. I'm not going to let him steal my happiness."

"But we don't know where the Tiger is."

"He'll certainly appear. I have to stop him—or he'll stop me."

"You don't need to kill him. You can return Uncle Bunny's money."

"He has to die. And if I die in the fight, then I'll die happy. Happy because I know I love you and I know you love me."

The girl embraced him, threw her head down onto his shoulder, and wept. Ajo Kawir returned her embrace, stroked her back, and comforted her with gentle pats.

—

The two kids were walking on a rocky road that connected the main drag with Ci Jaro village. They stopped at that same food stall by the side of the road. Those two *ojek* weren't there this time, maybe they were taking some passengers somewhere, but the woman who owned the food stall was there.

"I already told you that if I knew where the Tiger was I'd make him pay me back."

"That's bullshit," said Ajo Kawir. "He's rich. There's no way he owes money at this food stall."

"He owes me money. The last time he showed up here he forgot to pay. He told everyone to eat and drink on him, and then someone told him that a police squad was on their way to capture him and he left with a number of men, and he forgot to pay, and nobody else wanted to pay in his place. And since then he's never been back."

"Listen up, I'm really getting impatient, and if I can't kill the Tiger, then I just might have to kill someone *else* in this village."

———

The old man who opened the door after they pounded on it just stood there looking at them for a few moments. People said he was the Tiger's uncle. The cut of his jaw did not at all remind Ajo Kawir of the Tiger (whose face he had come to know well, after constantly scrutinizing the photograph Uncle Bunny had given him), but that's what people said and Ajo Kawir and Gecko had no other choice but to believe them.

"If you two find him," the old man said after a while, "I'll be happy to hear the news that you've killed him."

They'd never learn of the Tiger's whereabouts from his uncle's mouth. "Idiot," grumbled Gecko as they took their leave.

———

The four men were woodcutters, working on the edge of the forest. And they weren't just chopping down trees, they were also carving the tree trunks into square beams. They were working in pairs: two men stood on top of a trunk suspended three meters above the ground while the other two men were underneath, each holding either end of a big long saw. When Ajo Kawir and Gecko arrived, they stopped working and now the four of them stood looking at the two newcomers.

They were woodcutters but, more importantly for Ajo Kawir and the Gecko, they were the Tiger's men. Whenever the Tiger appeared, they were always there. Ajo Kawir and Gecko sized them up, and according to their estimate, the four were about their age, no older. Maybe they were in their early twenties, twenty-three or twenty-four at most.

They paid close attention after Ajo Kawir said he wanted to see the Tiger and that they'd better not try to hide whatever they knew about his whereabouts. Ajo Kawir said, "The Tiger is nothing but a pathetic coward and loser if all he dares to do is send his boys to try to intimidate people." He wanted to meet the Tiger and finish their business.

And when, finally, Ajo Kawir said he'd kill any friends of the Tiger if the Tiger wouldn't show his face, one of them stepped forward with a big hatchet in his hand.

Ajo Kawir immediately pulled out a dagger from inside his shirt. Gecko took his out too. They got ready.

The man in front of them brandished his hatchet. Ajo Kawir and Gecko clutched their daggers tighter.

Another of the four woodcutters, who appeared to be the oldest, now advanced and ordered his friend with the hatchet to retreat. Then he looked at Ajo Kawir and Gecko, gesturing for them to put their daggers away.

"You aren't the only ones looking for the Tiger. Go home. I promise you, if there's any news from the Tiger, I will come deliver it to you personally."

Ajo Kawir and Gecko put their weapons back under their shirts.

—

Iteung opened the box that had just arrived from the printers. It was filled with their wedding invitations—they were practically shining. She had already checked the layout and design before they were printed, but now she checked them again. It was as if she didn't really believe it was her name printed there. Ajo Kawir looked at her glittering expression. He saw her little smile. Iteung peeked over at him, and that glance made him fall in love all over again. Time and time again he had fallen in love with that girl, for these simple things. He returned her smile, and promised himself that nothing would stop their happiness. He felt like a truly lucky guy.

—

Five guys. They tried to stop his happiness. They waylaid him in the street, walking home alone from Iteung's house. He didn't recognize them, but they certainly recognized him. He didn't have a problem with taking them on, but five guys are still five guys, and only in kung fu movies did one fighter easily defeat five opponents.

Ajo Kawir collapsed to the sidewalk. One of the guys, who revealed his name to be Good Budi, crushed the five fingers of Ajo Kawir's right hand with his hard-soled boot. Ajo Kawir yelped as his fingers swelled and split and blood trickled out, but that same boot stopped his cry with a kick to his jaw.

My fingers, he thought. My fingers belong to Iteung. My fingers are what give her pleasure. You shithead.

Ajo Kawir tried to get up, but five guys are still five guys—five guys who knew how to fight. They left him curled up in the gutter. Not one part of his body could be convinced to rally.

"Don't try to fight back," said Good Budi. "You should never cross the Empty Hand—you know that."

—

Iteung could hardly believe the Empty Hand would do that to her beloved. She was friends with them, she said while bandaging Ajo Kawir's hands. A city minibus driver on his way home had seen him lying by the side of the road, and had dragged him inside his vehicle, asking him which hospital he wanted to be brought to. Ajo Kawir didn't want to go to a hospital, he just wanted to be taken to his sweetheart's house.

"They said they were from the Empty Hand."

"But who were they, exactly?"

"I don't know," said Ajo Kawir, grimacing at the aching and stinging pain throughout his body. The fingers of his right hand were the most gravely injured—they were a purplish blue, but he felt lucky that at least none were broken. "One of them, I think he was the leader, said his name was Good Budi."

"Who?"

"Good Budi."

"*Shit!*"

Ajo Kawir rarely heard Iteung curse, and he was happy to hear it. He reached for her hand, lifting his head and then resting it in her lap.

"I'll take care of that asshole myself," she said. "Shit."

—

"Leave Iteung. Don't claim her as your woman, and don't even think about marrying her. The best thing for you to do, if you want to live, is to leave her right now." That's what Good Budi said after he'd introduced himself, a moment after he'd intercepted Ajo Kawir on the sidewalk. The other four guys had stood behind him, opening and closing their fists as if getting ready for a fight.

"And who are you to forbid me from marrying my own girlfriend?"

"I'm the one who's been looking for you, who called you the other day, the one who's going to make your wedding day nothing more than a dream that will never come true—the one who will make you suffer. You'd better pray that today is not the day you die."

"And why don't you want me to marry Iteung?"

"Because she belongs to me. She's my lover, she's my girlfriend. Because she's going to marry me, and have my children."

Damn—and I thought all this was about the Tiger, Ajo Kawir said to himself. But it turned out he'd gotten mixed up with a jealous kid.

Good Budi was more like a mama's boy than someone bold enough to challenge another guy to a fight by the side of the road. His four friends looked way tougher than he was. At first Ajo Kawir wanted to laugh at the whole ludicrous affair. He looked at Good Budi: his face was pale, with a few soft wisps of hair growing on his upper lip—he couldn't even grow a mustache yet. His hair, slicked back and shiny with product, reminded Ajo Kawir of a cheesy actor.

Ajo Kawir had been ganged up on a few times before, by groups of three or four guys, so he wasn't afraid of being outnumbered. He had been beaten black and blue, and he had also made his opponents suffer. But five guys were still five guys.

Ajo Kawir looked at Good Budi and the four others and once again he wanted to laugh at this farce. He wasn't afraid. If they wanted to fight, he would oblige them. But if they wanted to separate him from Iteung, he would separate them from their lives.

That was something else, a serious matter, one he himself would take dead seriously.

But then they took him down. He really should have been a bit more careful. Good Budi wasn't trying to kill him, not then. But he vowed he would kill him some other time. And members of the Empty Hand never went back on their word about something like that.

———

"Dammit," said Iteung. "He's not my boyfriend. I swear to God, I've never been with anyone else besides you."

"He said he was your lover. That he was going to marry you. And that you were going to have his children."

"Shit."

Iteung admitted that Good Budi was indeed a member of the Empty Hand. She had met him and gotten to know him at the academy, and it could be said that they were friends. He was the one who had most often given her work when the Empty Hand needed someone—Iteung had worked for them a lot, but never on a hit. Iteung had never killed anyone, though she had no problem roughing people up.

For a long time now, Good Budi had offered his heart to Iteung, but she wasn't interested in him at all. Still, he'd persisted in trying to win her over. He did all the things that a man in love would do: he called her on the phone, he invited her to go to the movies, he stopped by to visit, he sent her flowers, he gave her presents on her birthday, and declared his love for her over and over. And over and over, Iteung rejected his advances and refused to go out with him.

But Good Budi wasn't just persistent in declaring his love to Iteung: after a while, he also began to tell other people that Iteung was his girlfriend. Iteung was annoyed by that, and a number of times she had sought him out to tell him, angrily, that she most certainly was not.

———

"I think that now I have to go find him and close his mouth forever."

"What are you going to do?"

"Pound his mouth shut, of course."

"You can't go alone."

"I absolutely will go alone. You stay here—don't go anywhere until your wounds have healed."

"I can't. I can't let you go alone."

"I have to shut his mouth."

"I'll get Gecko to go with you. There were five of them. Five guys are still five guys. Wait for Gecko, then you can go."

———

A few months after Ajo Kawir's twentieth birthday, and a few days after Iteung turned the same age, they were married. Iteung's parents were overjoyed. Ajo Kawir's parents were also quite pleased. Iwan Angsa and Wa Sami's eyes welled up to see Ajo Kawir a groom. Gecko smiled at everyone as he joined in welcoming the guests.

Now Iteung belonged to Ajo Kawir and he belonged to her. Out of everyone, they were the happiest, and no one could upset their happiness. No one could stop their wedding.

But if there was one creature who didn't know how happy the day was, it was the pecker inside Ajo Kawir's pants. That bird was still sound asleep. Maybe he had forgotten that he was supposed to get up. If he had awoken, he would certainly have been happy too.

But he was still asleep. Sound asleep. And he didn't know that he was supposed to be celebrating.

Sorry, Bird, but because you are still hibernating, we're going to take your place and become happy creatures ourselves, said Ajo Kawir's fingers.

—

Good Budi came to their wedding. He embraced Ajo Kawir and said he wished them well. He also said, please forgive me for what I did a while back. Ajo Kawir smiled. That kind of thing happens all the time he said, returning Good Budi's embrace and patting him on the shoulder. On every wedding day there are some who are sad, but there are also always moments of forgiveness and mutual understanding.

Iteung and Gecko had quickly taken care of the business between the two men. A few days after Ajo Kawir was left in a heap by the roadside, they went to Good Budi's house. Good Budi and his four friends were there. They were all part of the Empty Hand, but Iteung was not afraid to face them and neither was Gecko.

Iteung shut Good Budi up good in just a couple of seconds, leaving his mouth swollen and split. Gecko repaid whatever had been doled out to Ajo Kawir, with Iteung's help of course—although none of the guys were left lying in the gutter, it was enough to settle the matter.

And now, Good Budi had come to their wedding. With a gift and a warm embrace.

—

As the wedding celebration was drawing to a close, Ajo Kawir saw Iteung chatting with Good Budi. They were laughing. Ajo Kawir smiled. Whatever the case, they were still friends. They had studied together at the academy for who knows how many years. They laughed, and Ajo Kawir smiled, watching them from a distance. He was happy that everything had worked out. He had been worried that other members of the Empty Hand would seek revenge, but now he felt that had just been him getting carried away.

My life might not be perfect. My penis can't get hard. But I just had a beautiful wedding. And I'm going to have a happy family.

At the age of twenty, with all that he had suffered, Ajo Kawir had turned into a wise philosopher.

—

"Have you washed your hands?"

"I have."

And so their wedding night was filled with beautiful and pleasurable finger play.

—

Ajo Kawir said that sooner or later they would have to move out of the house and find their own place. Iteung said, "We don't need to rush. Papa and Mama are happy with us living here. Plus," she said, "we don't have a lot of money.

"If the Tiger shows up, we'll have a lot of money. Enough to buy a house and open a small store."

"Shhhh." Iteung placed her index finger on Ajo Kawir's lips. "Don't think about that. Don't think about the Tiger. Forget it. I don't want you to get hurt again. I don't want anything to happen to you. I don't want to lose you. Stay here, by my side."

Ajo Kawir hugged her and kissed her, before laying her down on the bed.

—

"Darling, your nails are getting long. Would you mind trimming them?"

"Of course not."

Night after night, his fingers were getting more and more skillful. Ajo Kawir was growing ever more convinced that there were certain things that could only be done with fingers—nothing else could do what they could do.

—

They went to the nearest police station. After scoping the place out from across the street, they saw a cop lounging in the security booth.

"Excuse me, sir," said Ajo Kawir. "We're looking for an old friend, an officer who helped us out when we were attacked by a gang of youths after a *dangdut* concert. We want to thank him ...What was his name? Ah, that's the thing, we forgot. We're so dumb that we forgot to ask him his name."

"Yeah, I could tell you must be idiots from the way you look—before you were even born you were already cursed with stupidity," the police guard taunted them, laughing. "And how would you recognize this officer?"

"His one distinguishing feature," Ajo Kawir said, "is that he has a scar across his chin."

"Policemen come and go, moving from one territory to another, from one squad to another. I've never seen a policeman with a scar on his chin. I've only been here three years. Maybe he's at precinct headquarters."

Ajo Kawir and Gecko went to the precinct office and asked the same thing to the policeman on duty there. They were looking for an officer with a scar across his chin and his friend, about whom all they remembered was that he'd been smoking a clove cigarette, but anyhow after many years the two seemed to have disappeared without a trace. They got more or less the same answer. Maybe try the borough office, said the precinct officer.

—

"I've been thinking about this the past few nights. Maybe there is a way to make your bird stand up again," said Iteung.

"I've tried so many different things already, from the most painful to the most ridiculous. I've gone to see thirteen witch doctors and they all gave up."

"But if it's true that this all started that night, the night those two policemen raped Scarlet Blush and you saw them, just like you told me, then maybe …"

"You think that if I kill them in an act of revenge for what's been happening to me all these years, then my bird will stand up again?"

"I don't know, I'm just wondering."

"Gecko and I looked for them before, when we thought we could fight them, years after it happened, but they'd disappeared. I don't know where they came from, and if I knew, it's most likely that they have already been stationed somewhere else, who knows where. Policemen come and go; they get moved from one territory to another, like soldiers."

The conversation ended there. For a few moments they were both silent, until Iteung approached Ajo Kawir and embraced him.

—

She touched him, caressed him. She knew the Bird wasn't going to stand up from that, but she still touched him, still caressed him.

Then she bent down and slowly began kissing the Bird. She stuck out her tongue and licked it, like a mama cat grooming her kittens.

"What are you doing?" asked Ajo Kawir.

Iteung just looked up at him, with the Bird between her lips.

"That's not going to make him stand up, and you know it."

"But I still just want to do it. Can't I?"

"You can, if you want to."

For a few moments neither of them said anything else. Then Iteung lay down on his chest, simply letting their hearts beat in unison. Not long after that, they talked about looking for the two policemen from Ajo Kawir's past, and the possibility of killing them.

—

He waited until afternoon, and finally Iteung appeared. Her face looked a bit pale. "I'm sorry," she said. "I forgot to tell you that I was going to a friend's house and she doesn't have a telephone. Have you already eaten?"

"Yes, I ate. But I'm worried that you haven't eaten. You look so pale."

"I'm fine. I ate two slices of bread."

"You have to eat rice."

Iteung smiled and kissed his lips. Ajo Kawir hugged her and kissed her back.

—

One morning, he saw Iteung shivering. He asked her what was

wrong. Iteung didn't reply and just kept shivering. She got out of bed and went to the bathroom. Ajo Kawir hurried after her asking, "Are you sick?" But Iteung didn't answer. She threw up in the bathroom.

Ajo Kawir prepared some warm water for Iteung, thinking that she wanted to take a bath. He also made some tea and brought it to the bed where Iteung was resting. He stood for a few minutes by the bedside but Iteung just kept lying there, curled up with her back to him.

—

Outside a light drizzle was falling. He saw Iteung half running from the road toward the house. Ajo Kawir hurriedly opened the door. Iteung ran inside. Ajo Kawir closed the door and then turned toward Iteung. She was standing there, looking back at him. They looked at each other for a few moments in silence.

Iteung's hair was damp, and so were her face and her clothes. But she still just stood there. After a few minutes, Ajo Kawir realized that her eyes were full of tears.

"What's wrong?" he asked. "Where have you been, since you left this morning?"

Iteung's tears streamed down her cheeks.

"Iteung! What's wrong?"

"I was just at the hospital," she said. She began to sob. "I'm … I'm pregnant."

"What?!"

Iteung pushed past him, slumped forward, and collapsed on the sofa. She wept and hid her face. In between her sobs she said something, but Ajo Kawir couldn't make it out.

"Iteung!" he began to shout. "Tell me who? Who?"

Iteung's shoulders shook.

"You whore!"

Ajo Kawir turned, opened the door, and went out into the drizzle, slamming the door behind him.

—

"We met while chopping wood in Ci Jaro. Just like I promised I would, I've come with news of the Tiger. The Tiger said he doesn't want to fight you. He hasn't fought for a long time. He's not in that world anymore."

Ajo Kawir looked at the guy with red eyes and gnashed his teeth. "I don't care. I want to fight him. Tell the Tiger he has to fight me."

—

With his body drenched and shivering, Ajo Kawir curled up in a corner of Wa Sami's grocery store. No one could get him to talk, until Gecko appeared and sat down in front of him. "I want to beat someone up," said Ajo Kawir.

—

Finally, he met the Tiger. And it was true—but the Tiger hadn't just stopped fighting, he *couldn't* fight any more. One of his legs had been amputated. He was armed with nothing but a crutch, and old age had already eaten away at all his past fury. But Ajo Kawir didn't care. He wanted to beat someone up. He had come to fight.

Ajo Kawir grabbed the crutch. The Tiger staggered, but before he collapsed, the crutch whammed against his skull. The crutch cracked and broke, as did his skull, which split open like a hacked up coconut shell.

"Whore!"

❈ 5 ❈

HE HAD THOUGHT that he would find serenity on the road—a peace that would come from the wheels turning, the landscape running by on his left and right, the song of the wind. A peace rising from the whirr of the engine and the tires rolling across the asphalt. He was wrong, of course. The road didn't give him any peace at all. And that became only more evident when that woman Jelita suddenly appeared, making him mumble to the kid, "We've got a big problem."

———

The guy driving the sedan was clearly insane. He passed the truck on the left, going almost eighty kilometers an hour, using the pebble-strewn shoulder because the right lane was filled with heavy traffic. At first, the truck driver didn't notice what was happening. In front of them the road was getting narrower, rising a bit toward the bridge. There was only a little bit of open space in between the truck and the guardrail, but the sedan was forcing its way through until the driver realized his car wouldn't make it and hit the brakes, wheels scraping against the rocks—if he didn't, he would slam into the guardrail, or ram into the truck's undercarriage. The truck driver also slammed on the brakes, making his truck shudder violently, because if he didn't he would squash the sedan.

The sedan screeched to a stop a mere inch from the guardrail, while the truck stopped with its nose practically touching the sedan, just a few inches away. For a few moments both vehicles were perfectly still. The traffic in the right lane slowed down as the drivers looked over at them, wondering what would happen next.

The driver of the sedan got out. He was about forty, balding. He stomped over to the truck and came to stand in front of it, peering up into the cab. He was carrying a hockey stick, which he pointed in the truck driver's face.

"You bastard!" he yelled. He made as if he wanted to smash the truck with his stick.

"If you want to, you could beat that baldy up," said the *kenek* sitting in the passenger seat, a kid of about nineteen named Gaptooth Mono. "You wouldn't be in the wrong, that guy is a super asshole."

Ajo Kawir looked at the *kenek* and thought, eleven years ago, when I was his age, I would have done just what he's suggesting, maybe worse. In fact, he was sure that if this had happened eleven years ago, he would have let his truck smash Baldy's sedan. But he wasn't going to attack Baldy now, because it wasn't necessary.

"Or how about you let me get out and beat him up for you?" Gaptooth Mono said, still looking for a fight.

"I don't want you to make trouble, kid," said Ajo Kawir. "Let's just smile and say we're sorry. The whole matter will be settled and we can continue on our way. No trucks will get damaged, no sedans will get wrecked, and more importantly, nobody will get hurt. We should be thankful that neither of us went plunging into the river."

"I want to beat that bald jerk up."

—

Not long after he was released from prison, during one of his gigs driving his truck from Cirebon to Madiun, Ajo Kawir saw Gecko. Gecko had taken Wa Sami's advice to move to Yogyakarta and go to college. Of course his studies had been a bit neglected—that is to say, a total wash—but he'd decided to stay there.

"I've begun to understand what my privates want."

"And what does your bird say?"

"He is choosing the way of tranquility. Like a Sufi. Like a Grandmaster. This bird is taking the path of silence and solitude. He sleeps soundly and peacefully, and I have learned from him."

"And what exactly have you learned from this bird?"

"To live in silence and solitude—without violence, without hate. I've completely stopped fighting. I've really taken its message to heart."

Gecko was determined not to laugh. When they parted, Gecko thought, if the Bird was following a path of silence and solitude, the path of a Grandmaster, maybe it wouldn't be long before the Bird would learn how to read the holy book and start giving sermons. Imagining that, he laughed silently to himself.

—

Gaptooth Mono sat there reclining and starting to doze off. His eyes blinked open and looked up at the truck's ceiling, where he had fixed a picture of a girl about his age, whom he called his sweetheart. Without looking over at Ajo Kawir, who was busy driving, he said: "Tell me about that guy you killed. What was his name? They only said that people called him the Tiger."

"That's all nonsense. I never killed anyone. I never fought."

"Don't lie. People said that you used to be a fighter for hire and you killed someone. You went to jail because you killed someone."

"Don't believe everything you hear, kid. That's enough. If you want a chance to drive later while I rest, then you should go to sleep now. If you're still drowsy, I won't let you drive."

The kid didn't say anything else. He fell asleep. Ajo Kawir looked over at him and smiled. He smiled at the picture of the girl on the roof of the truck. He had a photo like that too, right above his head, also affixed to the ceiling. It was also a picture of a girl, but one who was younger than the kid's sweetheart. She was a child, barely eleven years old.

—

There were plenty of young guys about his age, in their late teens or early twenties, who became *kenek*, assisting drivers with their haul and navigation and sometimes spelling them at the wheel, but whatever rest area they stopped at, he always looked like the youngest, maybe because his face was clean-shaven and a little bit pudgy, or maybe because of his innocent expression. Gaptooth Mono always tried to make up for his boyish looks with rough talk, insulting everyone and cursing at everything, and drinking as much hard liquor as he could hold—as long as Ajo Kawir had given him permission, usually only granted when they wouldn't be getting right back on the road the next morning.

In the middle of one night, they went to a coffee shop and sat down across from one another—often they'd sit with the others, but sometimes if there was an empty table the two of them would sit alone—and that was when the Beetle appeared. He wasn't very tall, but his body, covered in homemade dragon tattoos, was thick.

The Beetle appeared with three other guys, and when he saw Ajo Kawir and the kid at their table, he approached them.

The Beetle stood behind Gaptooth Mono and pressed his body up against his back. His hips thrust forward and soon began to move in a slow circle as he stroked the kid's shoulders. He smiled as he did it.

"How's it going, kid?" he asked.

Gaptooth Mono didn't reply. He was disgusted—he could feel the Beetle's dick pressing against his back. The longer it stayed there the bigger and harder it got.

This was already the third, or maybe even the fourth time it had happened. He couldn't take it any more. He wouldn't stand for any man's penis pressing against his back, rubbing and growing like that. He took a bottle of soy sauce and smashed it against the corner of the table. The neck of the bottle cracked, soy sauce splashed all over the table, and he stood up and turned around, brandishing the jagged edge of the bottle at the Beetle.

The Beetle jumped back just in time—if he hadn't, his stomach would have been ripped open.

"Hey, hey, good-looking. You want to have a little bottle duel with me, do you?"

The Beetle grabbed his own bottle of soy sauce from another table and smashed it just as the kid had done, looking back at him with a goading smile.

Ajo Kawir quickly stood and yanked on the kid's collar. He threw some money in the coffee shop owner's direction and nodded, to indicate that the money was for the drinks and the two bottles of soy sauce. At the door of the shop, Ajo Kawir grabbed the jagged bottle top out of Gaptooth's hand and threw it into the trash can. It clanged loudly as he dragged the kid toward their waiting truck.

—

"You know, you could have died, with your stomach split open and your guts spilling out everywhere," Ajo Kawir said. They were back on the road and he was driving, with the kid sitting next to him.

"That'd be better than having him do me in my ass—everyone knows he's buggered other *kenek*."

"Indeed, our genitals can move us with a savage power. They're like a second mind—a mind more influential than our actual brain. That's what I've learned from mine, after all these years."

—

When he was alone, squatting on the toilet, Ajo Kawir would look down at his penis quite often. Sometimes he'd smile and say, Hey, how are you today, Bird? If you want to keep sleeping, sleep as soundly as you want. I won't bother you.

This time, just as he expected, his bird stayed still and quiet. The longer he looked at it, the more it looked like the head of a lazy turtle.

It was as if it desired nothing from this world. It didn't want to get up, didn't want to stretch, didn't want to feel a woman's touch.

He had almost forgotten how long the Bird had been asleep. Twelve years? Twenty years? Just like it said in the Koran, God had made pious men sleep for hundreds of years in a cave—three hundred and nine years, to be exact. If in this world there was a wise and righteous member, he thought, smiling and laughing at himself, then it's this bird. This Grandmaster who is following a tranquil path.

—

The truck behind them pulled up close, riding their ass. Its horn honked, loud and aggressive. It seemed like it wanted to pass them, but that was impossible in such heavy traffic.

Ajo Kawir was driving his truck a steady sixty kilometers per hour. Apparently that was annoying the truck behind them. He sped up to almost seventy. That was already too fast for a truck on a bad two-lane road with the opposite lane jammed with traffic, but he accelerated a little more, hoping he could put a little more distance between them and that truck.

No such luck. The truck that was following him sped up too, tailing him impatiently. Again the horn honked, over and over, growing fierce.

Gaptooth Mono looked back and muttered, "Shit. It's the Beetle."

—

A few weeks ago, they'd been in a truck terminal in Pluit, in the northern part of Jakarta. That's where they usually waited for their next load. They were willing to transport just about anything, as long as they were getting paid enough and the goods wouldn't get them arrested or topple their truck, but in those days, that didn't really leave much for them to transport.

While waiting for their trucks to get packed up, the drivers would kill time sitting in food stalls and coffee shops—smoking, drinking coffee, and watching television. If they had a little extra money they'd drink beer. If they had a little more than that, they'd take a whore into their truck cabin or out back behind the food stalls.

Ajo Kawir and the kid were sitting on a small bench next to a food stall, drinking beer. That day, Ajo Kawir had said that they could both drink. We're not going to get a full load for two days, I guarantee, he said.

Then the Beetle appeared. They had seen him a few times before—he was usually at another terminal, but he occasionally showed up here—but this was the first time they'd heard him talk.

"You don't have to be a tough guy to kill the Tiger, any weak old granny could do it."

Gaptooth Mono's face flushed red, but he saw that Ajo Kawir was just sitting there, calmly sipping the cold beer in his glass.

—

Ajo Kawir kept driving the truck at a steady speed, just a little over seventy. He couldn't go any faster than that. He didn't want to plunge into a ditch or crash into one of the huts lining the two-lane road.

The Beetle's truck kept tailing him. Sometimes he'd draw so close that he was only a few inches behind, then he'd slam on the brakes and release them again. Again he honked his horn, flicking his brights on and off.

Ajo Kawir tried to give him some space, moving his truck over just a little to the left. The Beetle tried to pass, moving to the right, but there wasn't enough room. A bus was approaching in the on-coming lane. Slamming on the brakes, the Beetle moved the truck back to the left.

In his rearview mirror, Gaptooth Mono could see the truck behind them rocking from left to right. He thought that if Ajo Kawir just tapped the brakes, the truck would slam into their back bumper. If he was driving, he thought, he wouldn't hesitate to do it.

—

That first day, Ajo Kawir was sitting in the driver's seat. The truck was full with a load ready to be taken to Medan. He liked the route from Jakarta to Medan, the haul would be good and the pay even better. He might be carrying washing machines, photocopiers, or rice cookers. He didn't have to worry about that kind of load spoiling on the way. He might even be able to give himself a bonus—he was transporting some sacks of motorcycle helmets that he had stuffed in with the other goods. We're going to install a new stereo to turn this truck into a good time, he promised the kid. Even so, he hated the return route from Medan to Jakarta. The haul was never good and the pay was even worse. Usually the truck was filled with bananas, nothing but bananas.

Someone banged on the door of the truck. He looked. The Beetle.

"You took my haul!" the Beetle yelled.

"What do you mean?"

"Those sacks of helmets belonged to me. You took them from me. Get out right now, and unload those helmets, Asshole."

Ajo Kawir came out of the cabin. The other drivers and *kenek* at the terminal drew near. They wanted to see a good fight.

But there was no fight that day. Ajo Kawir took the Beetle to see a young Chinese guy sitting in his car in the parking lot with his wife. They looked like newlyweds, and maybe they had just started their business supplying helmets to a few stores in Medan. They got out of the car.

"The helmets belong to them, and they gave me the haul. Here's the receipt with their signatures," Ajo Kawir said, waving the piece of paper in the Beetle's face.

"But the guy offered the job to me," the Beetle said. He was pissed off—he hadn't thought that Ajo Kawir would actually bring him to the couple.

"Your price was too expensive. He gave us a cheaper price," the wife said. Her husband seemed a little pale and nervous, but she was keeping her cool.

"Well I'll give you the cheaper rate now," said the Beetle. He glared at the husband.

"But we already made an agreement with him. He's going to haul our stuff." Again it was the wife who spoke.

The Beetle looked at the woman, staring her down, but she stared right back at him without blinking. In matters like these, women often have the bigger balls.

The Beetle finally left, grumbling. Ajo Kawir folded the receipt he'd been waving around and crammed it into his jeans pocket. Then he said to the couple, "You'd better get out of here. That guy is always looking for trouble."

The husband quickly yanked his wife back into their car.

—

"The Beetle is just looking for an excuse to start something," said Gaptooth Mono. He was gnashing his teeth.

"I know, but he's not going to get it."

"Sooner or later, he's going to challenge you to a fight over something. He doesn't like you, it's as simple as that. He doesn't like that people talk about you, saying that you're the one who killed the Tiger."

"He won't find any good reason to fight me, and I don't want to fight him—I don't want to fight anyone! I swear on my cock!"

—

The Beetle looked and saw the right lane was mostly empty. He moved his truck to the right and sped up. His left hand held the wheel, his right hand held down the horn. Now his truck was in the right lane, slowly gaining on the truck ahead of him. There were only a few centimeters between the two vehicles, and if they kept going this way his left rearview mirror would soon hit the right rearview mirror of the truck in front of him. He didn't care.

His *kenek* was clutching the edge of his seat, face pale and lips trembling. He had already asked the Beetle not to pass Ajo Kawir because there was no point—they weren't being chased, they weren't hauling a load that would quickly spoil. But the Beetle didn't listen.

He saw the truck in front of him slow down. He smiled and eased his right hand off the horn. If he could pass, then he would knock the truck to the left as soon as he had the chance, forcing it to slam on the brakes. And he would laugh.

That might lead to an argument, and maybe even start a fight. That's what he was waiting for.

Suddenly he saw a sedan speeding toward him in the oncoming lane. His truck was just about halfway past the truck in front of him. He estimated the distance between himself and the sedan, and how much time he would need to keep tailing Ajo Kawir's truck.

The Beetle pressed harder on the gas. His truck advanced faster. The sedan drew even closer. There wasn't enough time.

He took his foot off the gas and slammed on the brakes. He quickly swerved his truck left. Ajo Kawir had been trying to slow down and so the Beetle almost hit his back bumper, but he had to do it—if he hadn't, he would have slammed into the sedan advancing toward him, and then slammed into the pickup that was driving behind the sedan, and then two motorcycles behind the sedan, and maybe then slam into the bus that was behind the two motorcycles.

"Bastard!" he yelled.

He had to regain control of the truck, which was careening wildly. The truck in front of him pulled farther ahead. His hands shook and he punched the wheel in frustration. Then he smelled something bad.

"What stinks?"

"I ... pissed myself," his *kenek* said quietly.

"Bloody hell!"

—

He was often amazed at his own tranquility. The road had tested him many times, but he always stayed as calm as he pleased.

"Still, that's nothing compared to the Bird," Ajo Kawir said to Gecko when they met. "The Bird has seen the most beautiful pussy in the world, or at least according to me the most beautiful. He has received the most gentle caresses, the warmest kisses. But he stays quiet, he doesn't move. He lives in peace."

"I know," Gecko said. "I'm sure that even if a pair of scissors was cutting him in half, he still wouldn't move."

—

They stopped at a gas station. After filling up the tank, Ajo Kawir pulled his truck over into the parking area and went to the bathroom. Gaptooth Mono took his turn after Ajo Kawir got back.

They were sitting on the floor of the kiosk that sold diesel, their legs stretched out in front of them. They wanted to smoke, but they couldn't smoke there. Let's find a place to smoke and drink coffee, said Ajo Kawir, and after that you can drive and I'll sleep.

Night fell and soon they saw the Beetle's truck drive by. The kid spotted it with excitement.

—

Most truck drivers followed the more-or-less standard routes. If they lived in Sumatra, they would haul goods along the Jakarta-Medan route and back again. Sometimes they'd take a load as far as Banda Aceh, sometimes just to Bandar Lampung, following the same route. If the driver was from Java, he'd haul loads from Jakarta to Surabaya, or sometimes to Banyuwangi or as far as Denpasar in Bali.

But Ajo Kawir operated outside those rules of the game. He didn't mind going to other cities in Sumatra, and often hauled loads to various cities throughout Java. He was a man married to no particular city—he thought of the road as his home.

"We're a family of four, living in this truck."

"Four?" asked Gaptooth Mono.

"Yeah. Me, you, and the girls on the ceiling."

Gaptooth looked up at the two photos and smiled.

—

When they changed seats, the kid glanced up to turn on the light so he could organize all the stuff strewn about. The picture of the girl, who looked to be about eleven years old, caught his eye. He looked over at Ajo Kawir, who was trying to find the most comfortable position to sleep in the passenger's seat.

"Do you miss her?" the kid asked.

Ajo Kawir nodded, but then, peering over at the picture, shook his head. "I've never even seen her, except in this photograph."

"I know, you've said that a couple of times."

"And as for you, why is that girl's picture still stuck there? You think there's still hope?"

"Who knows," said the kid, starting the engine and turning off the cabin light. "I still love her."

"You're only twenty years old. In the next decade you'll fall in love with maybe ten different girls ... or maybe with a widow, or somebody's wife."

"Maybe," the kid said. He tested out the gas pedal and the brakes. "But right now, I only love her."

"Any specific plans?"

"I've thought about it a lot, but I'm not sure. I think one day I'll take her away with me. Maybe to Medan, maybe to Denpasar ... the point is, somewhere far away."

Ajo Kawir, quite sleepy, started to mumble, and that mumbling was the sign that he didn't want to talk anymore. But then he said clearly, "Don't kill me, okay? I don't want to wake up in the grave."

"Don't worry. If you die in this truck, you'll wake up in the stomach of a shark, because I'll throw your corpse into the ocean."

Ajo Kawir chuckled at that before falling asleep.

—

Gaptooth had never imagined he would become a truck driver. Not far from his house there was a copra-drying plant, where coconut oil was extracted from dried coconut kernels, and the owner had a truck. When he finished school he found work there, and he tried the truck out a few times. In fact, he learned how to drive a truck before he learned how to drive a car, but even so he didn't think he'd become a truck driver.

Ajo Kawir said that he was an amazing driver for a twenty-year-old. Ajo Kawir always said he could sleep soundly with Gaptooth behind the wheel. Being able to sleep comfortably while someone else was driving was the highest praise—Gaptooth Mono knew that, and he was proud. He promised he would never send Ajo Kawir to the grave.

—

The truck drove along peacefully. The kid looked at his speedometer, and he was happy with how fast they were going—not too fast, but fast enough for a truck with a full load.

They were heading east along the Northern Coastal route. It was the middle of the night, but there were still lots of vehicles on the road. He took a cigarette, slipped it in between his lips, and lit it. The smoke was quickly carried away by the breeze coming through the open window.

He put an Ebiet G. Ade cassette into the new stereo. They had bought it after carrying a sack of helmets to Medan a few weeks ago. He turned on the music and adjusted the volume. Not too loud, so as not to wake Ajo Kawir, but loud enough so he could hear its country twang over the noise of the traffic.

A truck pulled in front of him. In the glow of his headlights, he could see an airbrush painting of a half-naked woman and large letters spelling out: "After all the cold wind blowing in the streets, now I need to get me some heat." The kid smiled. He sped up a little bit, and when he got the chance, he passed. It wasn't the Beetle's truck, he thought, but there was no need to hurry, in about half an hour he was sure they'd see it.

—

The kid liked looking at the pictures painted on the trucks and the words that went with them—most were a little bawdy and made him smile, and some had religious messages, but out of all the ones he'd seen, he liked the picture and the writing on the truck he was driving best of all.

"I own this truck myself," Ajo Kawir had told him the first time they met, a number of months ago. "I paid it off over three years."

"You mean, you can buy a truck in installments using what you make from hauling loads as a driver?"

"I'm not too sure about that," Ajo Kawir said, laughing. "Before I went to prison, I had a lot of money and I used some of it to buy this truck."

Ajo Kawir said that he'd brought the truck to an art student in Yogyakarta—they'd been introduced by his friend Gecko, who loved to draw and paint. And the picture, so different from the ones on all the other trucks, was of a bird, sleeping so soundly it looked almost dead. But what the kid liked best was the motto above the sleeping bird: "Vengeance Is Mine: All Others Pay Cash."

—

The back of the Beetle's truck had a picture of Marilyn Monroe with small but legible writing: "It's a pity to let her go, but she's too expensive to keep."

They had passed six trucks, but he hadn't seen Marilyn Monroe yet. A half an hour had already gone by.

The kid kept on driving calmly; he'd smoked two cigarettes. Marilyn Monroe's not going anywhere, he thought, she's in front of me and I am getting closer to her, minute by minute. He was sure of it.

Underneath his calm exterior, his heart beat faster.

—

He'd felt this particular excitement before, when he was fourteen, walking down the school hallway, his heart beating faster with every step: walking toward him, still dozens of steps away, was the-kid-he-wanted-to-beat-up.

Classmates were milling about and he was staring into the eyes of the-kid-he-wanted-to-beat-up—soon, they would be even closer. They looked at each other for a few moments, then he threw a punch at his face.

I might lose, but I don't care, he has to feel my fists. He threw some more punches and the lip of the-kid-he-wanted-to-beat-up split. The-kid-he-wanted-to-beat-up was completely taken off guard, but after the third punch he began to fight back.

This one is for stepping on my shoes, this one is for tearing up my books, and this one is for the time you pulled down my jogging pants in front of the girls. Gaptooth punched wildly, and he took some wild hits too.

At first the other kids were too surprised to understand what was happening. Once they realized what was going on, the two boys were already black and blue, and with his face swollen, blood flowing out of his split lip, the-kid-he-wanted-to-beat-up was shoved up against the hallway wall. He himself had fallen head-first, with his school uniform torn and his nose bleeding. A few classmates broke them up, and a teacher appeared, escorting them both to the principal's office. The next thing he knew, his two front teeth had fallen out. That's how he got his name: Gaptooth Mono.

—

He could see Marilyn Monroe ahead of him, partially obstructed by a sedan whose headlights were illuminating the truck's rear end. He looked over at Ajo Kawir, who was sleeping soundly with his seat belt fastened. He looked back to the road, wondering whether the Beetle knew he was being followed or not.

Then the sedan passed Marilyn Monroe, quickly disappearing in front of it, and the kid stepped on the gas. The truck was now just a few yards behind Marilyn Monroe.

His heart was thundering, his memory filled with the-kid-he-wanted-to-beat-up back when he was still in school.

—

The Beetle yawned—the night was already two-thirds through and the road was beginning to get tiresome—and took out a cigarette. His *kenek* asked were they going to switch drivers now? The Beetle shook his head. "Later," he said. He still wanted to keep driving: "We'll stop at Ijem's food stall. I want to have a quick roll in the hay. I mean, what I really want is to buttfuck a boy but what can I do, all I can get is Ijem's piece."

He yawned again and then was startled by the blast of a strident horn, right behind him. He glanced into his rearview mirror. Another truck was driving just a yard or two behind him, swerving left and right, demanding some space, flashing its brights right up into his eyes.

"Bastard," he said under his breath when he realized who was behind him.

The Beetle moved his truck a little to the right without speeding up, deliberately blocking the road.

———

The kid knew the truck had cut him off on purpose. He didn't care, he kept on advancing, tailgating as close as he could get, blasting the horn and flicking his brights, over and over, so they'd shine right into the Beetle's rearview mirror.

Marilyn Monroe shifted to the right and then to the left, then zigzagged back and forth again. Her butt seemed to sway, hurling insults. Gaptooth Mono, pressing on the horn again, checked his speedometer and was surprised to see they were already going almost seventy, pretty fast for a truck carrying such a heavy load on a road that wasn't a proper highway, but he didn't care.

Because he'd been looking down at the speedometer, when the Beetle slowed down Gaptooth almost rammed into Marilyn Monroe's face, but his foot worked nimbly, easing up on the gas and slamming on the brakes—easing off, gunning it, easing off again, making the truck nod and bounce up and down.

"You monkey!" he cursed.

He looked over. Ajo Kawir was still sleeping soundly. His tranquility is really amazing, the kid thought.

—

"You could go to the dentist and ask him to put in a pair of false teeth," Ajo Kawir had once suggested to him.

"I'll never do that," Gaptooth Mono replied. "Those two teeth taught me something—they taught me to have balls."

—

Marilyn Monroe was now speeding on faster, as if challenging him to race. Fine, the kid thought, and sped up too, sticking just a few yards behind her, tailing her close.

"I might be about to lose two more teeth," he said to himself, "but I don't care. This is worth it."

When he tried to pass the Beetle's truck, it drifted to the right again before going back to the left. It kept on blocking him while the kid busily swerved right and left, trying to advance.

His eyes were fiercely glued straight ahead. He was no longer leaning on the horn. His hands gripped the steering wheel and his feet were in constant motion between the gas pedal, the brake, and the clutch. He was waiting for the Beetle to let down his guard, even just a little bit.

His opportunity only lasted a few seconds. The right lane was empty, and in front of him the Beetle had moved to the middle of the road, straddling the two lanes. But the kid saw a minibus coming in the opposite lane and behind it was a long stretch of empty road before the next vehicle. Marilyn Monroe would probably have to move back to the left to allow that minibus by, and so if he wanted to pass the Beetle's truck he'd have to do it at that exact moment, before Marilyn Monroe had the chance to move right.

As the minibus got closer, Gaptooth Mono floored it—Marilyn Monroe had the kid's truck right behind her.

The minibus brights were flashing urgently, and the kid was pleased that it was also speeding. If any of them made a miscalculation, all three could crash:

He clutched the steering wheel even tighter.

—

With the minibus upon them, the Beetle swerved his truck to the left, slowing down slightly, but the kid held his position—speeding up, even—knowing that although he was taking up some of the opposite lane, there was still enough space left for the minibus, if the driver wanted to use the shoulder. And he was sure that the minibus would.

The minibus driver did exactly that, and if the kid could have seen his face he would have seen how pale it was, with only a few centimeters in between his bus and that damned truck.

The road opened up a bit. The kid, going faster and faster, shifted completely into the right lane, cheek by jowl with the Beetle, facing oncoming traffic—he had to speed up even more if he didn't want to get boxed in.

—

Ajo Kawir had said his engine was better than any other truck's in all the depots and rest stops they'd been to. I'd never buy a truck with a crappy engine.

When he'd gone to Jakarta for the first time, he'd stayed at a body shop for a while. He hadn't known anything about motors before that, but unexpectedly, it turned out he enjoyed working on cars. Then, when he was in prison, he met a number of mechanics and he learned from them. The warden let him go in and out of the prison auto shop freely and fix the guards' cars.

"If you're into reckless driving," Ajo Kawir said, "you'll beat any other truck on the road with this truck."

—

Having slowed down, the Beetle needed some time to speed up again, and the kid easily pulled forward, aligning himself slowly but surely with the Beetle's truck.

The kid pounded on his horn again

This situation pissed the Beetle off. He moved his truck a little to the right, but the truck next to him kept advancing and if he moved any further, the two trucks would collide and both would crash.

After a few moments, the Beetle had regained his speed, but the kid was still going as fast as ever, and since he knew that the engine in that truck was way better than his, the Beetle only had one crazy choice.

The Beetle moved his truck over further to the right. Now both trucks were practically squashed up against one another. Meanwhile, a sedan was coming toward them. The Beetle smiled.

—

The driver of the sedan was a man of about thirty-five. He looked over at his wife sleeping deeply, and on her lap, their three-year-old daughter also sound asleep. "We'll be at Grandma's house in no time," he murmured, smiling.

He looked back at the road. Straight ahead, two pairs of headlights, which he could tell both belonged to trucks, were bearing down left and right. They were going too fast to suddenly hit the brakes. His lips began to tremble violently. Or maybe, he thought, we'll never make it to Grandma's house.

He released his foot off the gas and immediately slammed on the brakes. This sudden movement flung his wife forward and almost threw his daughter from her embrace. His wife awoke with truck headlights shining directly in her eyes—she screamed loud and long.

There was a little bit of space for the sedan to save itself from the truck onslaught, but the driver didn't want to take the risk. It was too close of a call, there might not be enough room, and in the second he had left, with his wife's constant screaming in his ears, he swerved to the left onto the stony dirt shoulder, stomping on the brake—the sedan shuddered and, rocking back and forth, screeched over the pebbles. He clutched the wheel as the car skidded almost fifteen meters before bouncing into the air and then crashing to a stop.

Both trucks had already disappeared into the night.

—

Only when the two trucks were almost neck and neck, with Marilyn Monroe just half a meter ahead, did the Beetle realize that the driver beside him wasn't Ajo Kawir, but the kid. He snarled, even more enraged, "That kid really wants to get fucked in the ass, and I swear I'm going to give it to him good, goddammit!"

But he had never seen a driver so reckless, almost running over a sedan, not giving an inch, just plowing straight ahead. He began to wonder whether he should start a slow retreat to save his own skin.

If the Beetle backed down, however, all the truck drivers in all the depots in Java and Sumatra would ridicule him. A truck driver for years, driving his truck in the left and proper lane, would surrender to a twenty-year-old kid who was driving his truck like a badass on the right? He would never be able to take the humiliation.

He wouldn't give up. He had to risk it. While the kid moved forward in the right lane, the Beetle pressed down on the gas and then swerved right, hoping to push the kid further right too. Far in the distance, he saw a line of cars coming toward them. The Beetle was sure that the kid would give up and be forced back behind him.

But instead the kid pressed on the gas and his left rearview mirror bashed into the Beetle's mirror, sending it flying, and leaving his own mirror bent.

"Bastard!" The trucks were so close the kid could hear the Beetle curse him.

Infuriated that the other truck was already a full meter ahead, the Beetle guided his truck back to the right.

At the same time, the kid nudged his truck to the left.

—

Until the final seconds, the Beetle still didn't believe that the kid was going to do it. He didn't know where the kid got the balls. He felt like the kid was pissing in his face, or worse. But the fact was, the kid did it.

—

The collision was unavoidable. The Beetle's front bumper slammed into the kid's trailer. The Beetle felt his truck shaking violently and he tried to turn right, to hold his position. But at the same time he felt—he truly felt—the kid turn to the left.

He saw sparks flying—

Bastard, bastard, bastard!

—

The string of cars in front of them was drawing closer. The kid was out of time. Still not slowing down at all, he pulled the steering wheel to the left once more. The truck shook and rammed the Beetle's truck, giving it a hard shove.

The kid worked to control his shuddering truck. He turned the wheel to the right, to the left, then to the right again and to the left again, all while working the brake.

At the same time, in the crooked rearview mirror, he saw the Beetle's truck tip off balance.

—

The Beetle gripped his steering wheel tightly, hoping to contain his momentum, but the kid's truck had rammed him so hard that one of his wheels was now on the shoulder, skidding over the loose rocks and pebbles.

His truck lurched, but the kid managed to merge into the left lane, just as the row of cars in the right lane passed by. The Beetle was trying to get back on the road, but his truck was going too fast: his wheels spun out and he knew he had lost control of his vehicle.

The Beetle realized that there was no use in trying to get his truck off the shoulder—if he forced it, the truck would flip over. He had only one last hope: the brake. He kept on pumping it lightly, again and again, knowing that if he pressed it too hard, he took the same risk of flipping.

But even then he couldn't save himself. His front left wheel skidded into a ditch and seconds later his truck slammed into the piling of a small bridge cutting across it, dislodging the bridge and dragging it a few meters before the truck finally came to a stop, its wheels suspended but still spinning, and its engine growling loudly.

He felt his whole body go weak. He inhaled the odor of piss, but he was too weak to say anything. All he could do was silently curse to himself, "Bloody hell."

—

"You can slow down now," said Ajo Kawir, opening his eyes. "There's no way he's still chasing you. I'm sure his axle is broken. And even if it isn't, he'll need a day to catch up with us, at the very least."

"Did you see that?" the kid asked. It turned out his face looked far from excited, more like a corpse come back to life.

"No, I didn't. But I felt it. I figured I needed to give you the chance to make him mad ... and I would be willing to swear on your two missing teeth that he is very angry now."

—

They decided to rest for a moment by the side of the road to calm down. It was almost dawn. They both got out and lit their cigarettes. Ajo Kawir inspected the damage and the kid leaned against an overpass wall, exhausted.

And that's when they heard the sound of someone puking inside the trailer. They looked at each other. Ajo Kawir went into the cabin, took a flashlight and climbed into the hold, pulling back the tarp cover. He scanned the inside with his flashlight, the kid standing beside him, and there, crouched among all the things they were hauling, they saw a woman retching, maybe thanks to having been tossed about by the kid's reckless driving.

Who knows why, but Ajo Kawir got a bad sense of foreboding. "We've got a big problem," he muttered. "A really big problem."

And that's how Ajo Kawir met that woman, Jelita.

❊{ 6 }❊

THEY BOUND HIM by his wrists and ankles to the four corners of the cot. Lying facedown and wearing nothing but a pair of gym shorts, he didn't move, didn't try to lift his head. The two men who had tied him up stepped back to the door of the cell. Soon after, an old blind man with a white cane appeared, approaching the cot: he ran his hands over the captive, feeling his muscles tense. A warden was just outside the cell, standing guard.

Without saying anything, Ki Jempes, the old blind man, flogged the bound man's back with the cane.

Ajo Kawir let out an earsplitting yell and writhed in pain. "Whore!" A red welt striped his back, his hands curled into tight fists, his muscles tensed even tighter, but he still kept his face buried in the cot.

Ki Jempes whipped his back again—once, twice, three times, with accelerating movements. Red marks crisscrossed everywhere on Ajo Kawir's skin, but he just muttered to himself, let out the occasional shriek, and cursed a few more times: "Whore! Whore!"

—

"Don't be stupid," said Uncle Bunny. "This is a good auto repair shop, you can learn about engines. Plus, you are safe here—they know you here. I don't want to see you die."

"You let Agus Cornpipe die."

That peeved Uncle Bunny. He didn't like people talking about that. Nevertheless, what Ajo Kawir said was true. He'd protected many scoundrels, just like his friends protected their own, but as he'd already explained to Iwan Angsa a number of times, certain things were out of his control. He hadn't wanted Agus Cornpipe to die, but others did: Agus Cornpipe would not apologize for what he'd done—and the thing was, he had slept with someone's mistress—so Uncle Bunny couldn't keep protecting him. I wouldn't like it if someone slept with my woman, and neither does anyone else, Uncle Bunny would say with a tone of annoyance. He tried to protect any number of people, but there was no way he could protect everyone.

"You don't need to protect me. You can wash your hands of me. I'm going away and if the Tiger's men want my life, they can take it. Easily. They can have it for free."

"Listen," Uncle Bunny said. This time his voice was loud and his gaze was stern. "I don't want to hear you arguing with me. You came to Jakarta because you wanted to stay alive, I don't want you leaving here to die in the street. I'm not just some ungrateful son of a bitch."

"Good. How long must I hide? Eleven years? Thirty-five years?"

—

They untied his wrists and ankles. Ajo Kawir dragged his body to the corner of the cell and collapsed there, shivering and sweating, his back splotched with blood. He was no longer screaming, bellowing, or spitting out curses and insults—he was just shivering.

One of the men who had tied him up grabbed a rag that the warden offered, to clean the cot—the blood was spattered everywhere, and it had to be gotten rid of.

"You all, go," said Ki Jempes.

The two men returned to their own cells; the warden took the cane out of the old man's hand and followed them. Now it was only Ajo Kawir and the old blind man, who reached into his pants pocket, took out a bundle of tobacco, and grabbed a few pinches. Even though rules can sometimes be disobeyed, the rule was that no smoking was allowed in the cell, and what's more, he didn't have a light. He sat on the cot chewing and didn't say anything, while Ajo Kawir just lay there curled up in the corner, shivering violently, before he lost consciousness.

—

"You don't need to keep hiding here forever. You also don't need to go and get caught on the streets by the Tiger's men. There's one place that's safe for you, and you'd only need to stay there for a couple of years. In my opinion, it would also help put out the flame that's burning you up inside."

"What place?"

"Prison. In any case, the police are looking for you—all you'd need to do is turn yourself in. I can make it so that you don't need to be locked up for decades. I think ten years would be good."

"The Tiger's cronies will murder me in prison."

"No, they won't. The jails are full of my men. They'll listen to what I say. And the Tiger's men will stop looking for you if they know that you're in there. Many of them are actually happy that you killed the Tiger. His own uncle wanted him dead, lots of his neighbors wanted him dead, and some of his men wanted him dead too, they just didn't have the guts to kill him themselves. If you're out on the street, they'll be forced to kill you in order to wipe the soot from their faces."

"Why is there soot on their faces?"

"Oh my God. That's why you should have gone to school, you idiot! That's just a turn of phrase from an Indonesian grammar lesson."

—

For more than an hour, Ajo Kawir lay in the corner and Ki Jempes chewed tobacco. The old blind man had already refreshed his chew a number of times and what he'd spat out was now splattered around on the floor. He'd just taken his fifth pinch of tobacco when he heard Ajo Kawir moan.

Ki Jempes looked over, as if he could see him.

Slowly, Ajo Kawir moved his body, lifted his head with effort, and with weak arms tried to prop himself up against the wall. When his back touched it he groaned and tried to stand, but then his body felt heavy and hurt everywhere. He collapsed to the floor again with a grimace, moaning some more.

"You'll get used to it, kid," said Ki Jempes. "And believe me, in a dozen years, when you get out of here, you'll miss it. "

—

I'm just a lizard on the ceiling of the cell. Waiting for a mosquito or a fly to pass by. I don't know what you all are doing down there, stripping this guy naked and then beating him with a cane until red lines shine on his back. All I know is how to catch mosquitos and flies, or more usually ants, they're the easiest prey. All I do is eat, and after that, expel the shit that's in my stomach.

Ah, just thinking about it makes me want to take a crap. My

134

stomach hurts. Maybe that mosquito I ate hadn't sucked enough blood. Pardon me, but my poop's about to slither out and fall.

———

The blind old man felt something cold splat onto his bald head. He touched it. Something mushy. He brought his fingertips to his nostrils.

"Dammit. I knew it was stinky lizard shit. Why did I have to smell it?"

———

Where the men bathed, there was a large and deep trough of water where they could scoop up water to wash themselves—or drown someone. Two men dragged Ajo Kawir there, thrashing and screaming, "Whore! Whore!" They paid no attention, shoving his entire head under water and holding it there for a while.

Ajo Kawir kept struggling to get free, but the two men held him down firmly. The water started bubbling around his head. His legs kicked. The longer he kicked the weaker he got, and then he stopped struggling.

Finally they pulled his head up, splashing water everywhere. Ajo Kawir opened his mouth wide, wheezing and panting, as if he wanted to take in all the air around them.

"Whore," he gasped.

He almost said something else, but the two men still had him and quickly sent his head back down underwater and held it there. Ajo Kawir thrashed about again. Underwater his eyes opened wide, bugging out. Air bubbles came from his mouth again, swirling around his head. His head shook back and forth, trying to free itself, but their grip on his hair was too tight. He writhed and kicked, this time even more forcefully. But the two men were really tough, giving no indication that they planned to let him go.

—

"Whore," he snarled at Iteung, who was kneeling on the floor in front of him, weeping and looking up at him beseechingly. He didn't want to look at her. In all honesty, he wanted to grab her hair and bash her head against the wall. Split it in two.

"Go ahead and kill me, if that will erase my wrongdoing," Iteung sobbed.

"You slut," he muttered, turning his back as if to leave her, but Iteung deftly grabbed his legs, hugging them tightly. Ajo Kawir almost toppled over—at first he kept trying to walk, dragging her along the floor, but Iteung, still sobbing, kept her hold on him, not wanting to let him go. He had the urge to kick her, stomp on her, but he knew that curled up inside her body was a little fetus. He could be a real asshole, but he would never hurt a baby.

Yet thinking about that baby—that fetus planted there by someone unknown—made the fire once again blaze in his head.

—

When they lifted his head up out of the water again, Ajo Kawir yelled as loud as he could, but the more he struggled the more firmly the men gripped him. Ajo Kawir roared again and, snarling, pushed one of the men, but the other one pulled back at him.

His eyes were bloodshot, red like the sky at dusk. His look seemed to say, let me go, or you both will die. But the men didn't seem at all intimidated, or maybe they didn't understand him. They gripped him even tighter and his eyes turned a deeper red—he snarled again. His muscles strained and he bellowed, struggling to free himself.

Without mercy, they once more thrust his head back down to the bottom of the trough. Water filled his mouth and nose. His body began to flounder. This time they held him down even longer. His chest was on fire, his lungs were about to explode—he couldn't hold on. When they finally let him go, he floated up to the surface of the water.

—

Ajo Kawir finally bent down and lifted Iteung up. At first she hung there limply, but Ajo Kawir held her upright. "Look into my eyes, Iteung," he said. He had to repeat himself a number of times— "Look into my eyes, Iteung!" Iteung kept her head bowed and her tears didn't stop. After he repeated himself again, Iteung finally raised her head and looked into his eyes, even though her gaze was blurry. "Do you love me, Iteung?"

That question started her crying again, even louder, and her shoulders heaved. But she nodded. Nodded with complete certainty.

"Good," Ajo Kawir said. "If you still love me, then let me go. Because if you don't, you'll make me into a fool and an idiot—even though, clearly, I am already an idiotic fool."

Iteung was racked with sobs, her eyes and cheeks swollen. But even so, she finally let Ajo Kawir go. He left without another word. Without looking back. Without any reassurance for Iteung that she'd ever see him again.

—

He sat alone on the night bus, his body weak. All his muscles felt like jello. Looking out the window into the darkness of the passing roadside with a blank stare, he could still hear the sound of a skull cracking open as it was hit with a wooden crutch. That crack bounced around inside his brain, overlapping with the sobs of his wife, as if the two events had happened at the same time, in the same place. The more he tried to get rid of those sounds, the louder they seemed. He rested his head against the window, closed his eyes, and now he saw the faces of the Tiger and Iteung.

"Where to, brother?" The conductor was standing next to him, asking for his fare.

Startled, he opened his eyes and looked up. For a moment he tried to figure out what the conductor had asked. The man repeated his question, taking out a bundle of tickets.

"Jakarta."

"But this is the bus to Surabaya, brother. You're going in the wrong direction."

He wanted to jump up. He wanted to get angry. He wanted to strangle that conductor's neck, push him and punch him. Make his nose bleed. Knock out his front teeth. But he knew he couldn't do any of that. His rage was already spent. He had absolutely nothing left inside.

—

Iteung would always remember those times—the bell signaling the end of the school day and the children making a racket trying to race each other out of the classroom. She'd be the last person to leave. Not because she didn't want to hurry out with the others but because their teacher, Mr. Toto, always asked her to wait a moment before going home, to help him with some small tasks. Those tasks were truly insignificant: separating the girls' homework books from the boys'; or going over the attendance books to see who'd missed the most school in the last month; or (this all usually happened on Tuesdays and Thursdays) adding up all the students' savings to see how much was in the class budget.

She would sit in her chair, pulled neatly into her desk, and Mr. Toto would sit beside her. The room would be quiet, the school deserted. While Iteung was completing her tasks, Mr. Toto would put his arm around her shoulder, and then his fingers would touch her breasts, with a naughty touch. And Iteung would look over at him, saying: "Hey, Teacher, what are you doing?"

Mr. Toto would chuckle and whisper, "Look, Iteung. Your chest is starting to grow. Pretty soon you're going to need to wear a bra."

Iteung had never thought of that, but she had noticed her breasts were indeed starting to stick out, even more than those of her class-mates. Mr. Toto liked to touch them. Sometimes he pretended that he'd done it by accident, but more often than not he clearly did it on purpose. Those touches made Iteung feel strange, but after a while she began to think that they actually felt good.

"Can I hold them, Iteung?"

"Teacher, don't."

But Mr. Toto's hands would already be inside Iteung's shirt, un-derneath her undershirt. Maybe those little mounds of hers only filled half of a handful, but they were solid and firm. Mr. Toto's hands would fondle and squeeze them. Iteung would almost squeal, but she'd hold it in. Her pencil would fall from her trembling hand.

—

Mr. Toto was holding Iteung close from behind. The man was sit-ting on a chair, embracing her, and Iteung was sitting on his lap. His left hand was holding the little girl's breast and the other hand was feeling around under her skirt. Iteung tried to get away, but Mr. Toto held her even tighter.

"Sir, let me go, sir."

"Just a minute, Iteung."

Mr. Toto's fly was already partly open. Iteung could feel something poking out insistently, touching her buttocks.

"Sir."

"Just a minute, Iteung."

Then she felt something wet and sticky. Mr. Toto's hands stilled and he stopped moving completely. Iteung quickly stood up, freeing herself, and looked back at the dark black genitals drooping on the chair.

"Sir."

"Go get that rag, Iteung."

Iteung felt a pain in the crack between her legs. She tried to walk like usual, but it hurt there.

—

Whenever she dreamed about that man, she would wake up dripping with sweat and her body would be hot, yet she'd be shivering. Her fingers would be trembling, her jaw would be clenched, but she could hear her teeth chattering.

At the same time, she was wet. Slimy. Flooded. As if she longed for that blunt piece of urgent flesh.

And Ajo Kawir would be startled when Iteung would wake up with racing gasps in the middle of the night. He would look over and see her face stippled with sweat. In the dim light, he could see she was pale. Ajo Kawir would grasp her hand, which felt cold.

"Iteung, what is it? What's wrong? Did you have a bad dream?"

Iteung would look over, and after a few moments she would smile. Ajo Kawir would wipe the sweat from her brow, her cheeks, and the tip of her chin, and Iteung would snuggle her body closer to him. Press her cheek to Ajo Kawir's cheek, then nibble on his lips. Ajo Kawir would kiss her lips in return.

Not long after that, he would feel her body grow warmer. Iteung's hand would reach for his hand, and then guide it to her underwear. Place it inside. Ajo Kawir's fingers would feel a thatch of hair, before finding the crack that was moist. Wet. Flooded. Iteung would squirm with pleasure.

—

"What are you dreaming about, really?" Ajo Kawir asked. They were sitting on the veranda, feeding Iteung's father's chickens. "You always wake up afraid. But at the same time, your pussy is wet."

Iteung looked at Ajo Kawir silently. It was as if she was trying to decide whether she should tell him or not. Finally, she said: "A big snake."

"A big snake?"

"As thick as a pillow, wrapping around me. I feel like I can't breathe, but then the snake wriggles around the soles of my feet. I'm scared, but at the same time …"

"Oh, I get it."

Then they fell silent, watching the chickens peck at the rice they'd thrown. They were holding hands. Iteung's head was on Ajo Kawir's shoulder. Then Ajo Kawir glanced over at her and Iteung smiled.

"Why are you smiling all of a sudden?"

"I'm wet," Iteung said, as a tinge of red appeared on her cheeks. "Again."

—

"Get up, you son of a bitch, get up!" But the Bird still didn't want to get up. The Bird wanted to be a stubborn S.O.B., wanted to be a hopeless lazy fool. It didn't care that Iteung wanted him desperately.

—

Remembering all of that reignited the flame in Ajo Kawir's chest. He snarled, which woke the old blind man—they were in the same cell, sharing the same cot. Ajo Kawir sat up, still snarling. He got up from the cot, walked a few steps, and his snarls grew louder, turning into low yowls. He stopped near the wall, his hands raised, and then his fists swung against the concrete walls of the cell. Their thuds echoed throughout the cell. The walls shook. Blood dripped from his knuckles.

Ki Jempes sat up in bed. He didn't say anything, just listened.

Ajo Kawir yowled again, this time louder. Then he began to let out a yell each time his hands slammed against the wall. The concrete now was flecked with red, and he screamed and screamed, pounding the wall. His shouts reverberated throughout the entire prison. Then footsteps.

A warden appeared, opened the cell door, and his two men grabbed Ajo Kawir. He tried to get away from them, tried to keep pounding his fists into the cell wall, but the men held him, firmly dragged him away, and threw him back down on the cot. The warden held out a cane to the old blind man. The two men held Ajo Kawir facedown on the mattress.

With one swift blow, Ki Jempes flogged Ajo Kawir's back with the cane, and he groaned again, and screamed.

—

The room was called the "Guidance Office." Mr. Toto came to get Iteung from class and brought her there.

Iteung entered the room with the palms of her hands feeling cold. The room felt cold too. Ghostly and dim. He sat down.

"Why do you keep avoiding me, Iteung?"

142

"I'm not, Sir."

"Oh, you, come here for a minute!"

With slow steps, Iteung began walking toward Mr. Toto. He immediately grabbed her hands and yanked her—Iteung stumbled and found herself straddling Mr. Toto's lap, her two small breasts pressed firmly against her teacher's chest. She tried to stand up, but Mr. Toto held her tightly. She could feel something firm and pointing upward, jabbing right into the opening of her own crotch.

—

"Papa, I want to take some extra classes," the girl said to her father, who was listening to a drama on the radio. Her father was a bit dazed, lost in the story, and turned to her distractedly.

"Oh, so it turns out my daughter has a little bit of initiative! What kind of classes do you want to take, child? Piano? Dance? Flower arranging? Sewing?"

The girl shook her head. She stood in front of her father with a determined look and lightly clenched fists.

"No? Don't tell me you want to take soccer or guitar. You're a girl! How about you take a baking class, and you can learn how to make cookies?"

The girl shook her head again.

"Or maybe you want to get tutoring? Math? English?"

Again she shook her head. Her fists clenched tighter.

Now her father wasn't paying any attention to the radio. He leaned over a bit to get a better look at his daughter. "So what kind of class do you want, Iteung?"

"I want to learn how to fight."

—

The Kalimasada Silat Academy was not far from the public hospital. Its name, as everyone knew, was taken from the Mahabarata. The Kalimasada was a holy book full of mystical knowledge, coveted by many but owned by Yudhistira, leader of the Pandawas. The academy's founder, Kyai Abdul Kadir, was a veteran of the twelve-year civil war between the republican army and Islamic rebels; the most elusive commander, he had controlled the entire jungle along the southern coast of Java, starting in Cilacap and continuing through Pangandaran, Parigi, and Cijulang, all the way to Port Ratu. When the republican army captured the rebel leader R. M. Kartosuwirjo and the morale of his militias collapsed, the guerilla commanders surrendered one by one.

Some were executed, while others spent their days in jail before being pardoned. Some came out of prison to find the world had changed. They had no work and no place to live, so they became robbers and thieves, or at least market "security"—in other words, petty extortionists. Most of them were friends with the republican army soldiers who had captured them, and as robbers and thieves, or at least petty extortionists, they needed armed protection, and the soldiers were there to protect them.

Kyai Abdul Kadir tried to rehabilitate these men. Some of them had been his soldiers in the jungle, and most of them had been just snotty-nosed kids when they joined the guerillas. He founded the Kalimasada Silat Academy to gather them together, to teach them not just self-defense, but also religious wisdom, and more importantly to give them a way to make a living. He knew all too well that it wasn't easy for former child soldiers who had grown accustomed to the guerilla way of life.

But only a few of them actually wanted to join the academy. The other ex-guerillas decided to make their own way, consorting with the soldiers, who sometimes needed their manpower to keep the peace—or disrupt the peace, as the case might be. Once the soldiers didn't need these kids anymore, they would just kill them. Kyai Abdul Kadir had predicted this, and the academy was one small effort to prevent such a sad fate. Luckily, he didn't have to see how the soldiers suddenly turned on the ex-guerillas and exterminated them. He died of old age before that happened.

—

The academy fell to the hands of his son. Even though this son had joined him as a guerilla—was, in fact, born in the jungle—he didn't have his father's deep religious knowledge and he cancelled all the religion classes. And while his father had taught the students how to sew, cultivate the land, and even manage loans in case they wanted to to start a small business, his son no longer gave any thought to how the students were supposed to be making a living. The Kalimasada Silat Academy turned into just a regular old martial arts academy. The students went there because they wanted to learn how to beat people up effectively, and because they wanted to know what it felt like to have courage.

A young girl stood at the enrollment table. When the guy signing people up asked for her name, she replied assertively: "Iteung."

"Why do you want to learn how to fight?"

"I want to be able to protect this." And she gestured down between her thighs.

—

Iteung was running around the outer edge of the soccer field. Most of the others had already stopped running—some of them were standing off to the side, some of them were walking—but she kept running. She had gone around more than fifty times, and her feet were still following one another. She had vowed that today she would go around seventy times.

Her legs were tired, but she would say to herself: you'd better keep running, Legs, because that's what I want you to do. She would never let her legs get whiny and protest. She would force them to do her bidding. She would never forgive herself if she had to stop or even walk before the last lap she'd planned. She would complete her rounds unless she died in the process.

"That girl is frightening," said her teacher, watching her from a distance.

—

Good Budi gave her a kick, right in her jaw. She didn't just career backward, her chin split and her lip was bleeding. She collapsed on the ground but she was only there for a few seconds, before jumping up again, wiping the blood away with the back of her hand. Then she walked—staggering a bit—toward Good Budi.

"Why aren't you fighting in earnest?" she asked. "I hope you're not fighting like such a chickenshit just because I'm a girl."

Good Budi sneered. *Okay,* he thought. He put up his fists, and the girl before him squared herself off as well.

As all their friends witnessed, standing in a circle in the large field out behind the academy, Good Budi once again assailed the girl, kicking and punching with escalating force. The girl was able to dodge some blows, but most of them landed. Her face was already black and blue, and her lip was swollen.

"I haven't lost until I've collapsed and can't get up again."

I'll knock you over so that you won't be able to get up for a week, thought Good Budi. But with that thought he actually let down his guard a bit, figuring the girl was already spent. Before he realized what had happened, just one surprise kick got him right in the nose, and Good Budi toppled to the ground. And the girl was already on him—her punches, all right at his nose, came in a fast whir, and then Good Budi fainted.

"This girl is really, really, frightening," Iteung's teacher muttered to himself again, before ordering a few people to tend to his two students.

———

"In very little time, you're already more of an ace than I am," Good Budi said.

They were sitting next to one another on empty stadium seats, tired out from running. Iteung just bowed her head in reply, with a little smile.

"I will always remember how I fought you, and how you fought back."

Iteung smiled again. She bowed her head lower, trying to hide the rising blush on her cheeks. It was as if something was coursing through the bottom half of her body, starting between her thighs.

Good Budi's hand touched her hand. She was surprised and drew her own back, but Good Budi's hand got hold of it again. Clasped it. Iteung fell still. She felt something flowing even more insistently in between her thighs.

She wanted to pull her hand away, but Good Budi's grip felt warm. She could fend off any blow, but she didn't know how to resist a warm touch. She emboldened herself to look up, and when she did Good Budi's face was right in front of hers. Good Budi kissed her lips. Iteung was surprised, and wanted to draw back. But another kiss was already coming. It felt warm, and she let it happen. She tried to hold back whatever was rushing through the lower half of her body, but it couldn't be contained.

Then she felt something touch that part—the part that was already wet. Good Budi's hand. She opened her eyes before she even realized that they'd been half-closed, and then she realized that Good Budi's hand was in between her thighs. Touching the wet cleft there, touching it with warmth and passion.

She felt like she was flying.

—

She stood at the door of the Guidance Office. Mr. Toto looked over at her, a bit surprised. They just stared at each other for a few moments, neither saying a word. Finally, it was Mr. Toto who opened his mouth.

"Ah, Iteung, where have you been all this time? Ever since you changed schools, you haven't come to see me. You're all grown up now."

Iteung smiled shyly. She came in and closed the door. Mr. Toto looked at her.

"Do you miss me?"

A bit taken aback, Mr. Toto nodded. "Of course. Of course I do, Iteung."

Iteung sat next to Mr. Toto, reached for his hand and held it. Mr. Toto didn't do anything in response, but glanced at her out of the corner of his eye. Then Iteung tilted her head and rested it on Mr. Toto's shoulder. The man felt his heart pounding in his chest and he tried to calm himself down. He wrapped his arm around Iteung, half embracing her. She looked at him. The tips of his fingers began to caress her breasts, which were now quite round and full. The girl glanced at him again. She touched Mr. Toto's pants. His shaft was already rock hard.

At first Mr. Toto didn't move as Iteung unbuttoned his shirt and took off his undershirt. But then he couldn't control himself, his hands reached for Iteung and began to undress her. Am I dreaming? he wondered. He had almost forgotten this girl—and now she was right there, she wanted him. His cock was impatient, erect and pointing toward Iteung.

He almost touched the girl, ready to engulf her body, but Iteung moved much quicker. One hard kick landed right on his balls. Mr. Toto shrieked, but his shriek didn't get all the way out because another blow slammed into his jaw, and then more kicks and punches came. He couldn't escape. In just a few moments, the man collapsed next to the chair legs, with a swollen nose and blood in the hand clutching at his balls. Sprawled out unconscious.

The girl calmly collected her clothes and put them back on. After gathering up Mr. Toto's clothes as well, she left.

—

Near the school gate there was an old asphalt drum that functioned as a trash can, where they'd burn garbage. There were still a few small flames flickering inside. Iteung threw Mr. Toto's shirt, undershirt, pants and tighty-whities inside. Slowly, the embers began to eat through them.

—

The schoolchildren were leaving their classes in small groups when someone shouted and pointed. The kids stopped in the middle of the yard, looked over, and then together they all shouted. In unison, they all pointed.

A teacher was coming out of the Guidance Office, stark naked. He seemed confused, staggering a bit, with a dazed look on his face. But then he came to his senses. He realized that he was naked in the middle of the schoolyard, in the midst of a crowd of screaming schoolchildren. Some of them were screaming because they were scared, others because they were amused at the sight of a pair of black genitals dangling from a thick forest of hair that looked like it hadn't been trimmed in months.

Their teacher was shocked to discover the condition he was in. He hurriedly covered both his eyes with his hands. He didn't seem to care that his privates were hanging there, swinging back and forth for all of the students to see—at that moment he had to shield his own eyes. He didn't want to see the world.

—

Iteung sat down on the bathroom floor, her teacher's black cock still playing in her mind's eye. The muscles at the bottom of her womb were throbbing. I want that black bird. Damn, I want that ugly black bird so bad.

This was a fight that she wasn't going to be able to win.

—

Iteung was sitting astride Good Budi's naked body. Just like his name, he was in fact a good guy. Obedient. If Iteung told him to lie still, he would lie still. And if he lay still, Iteung would move, with a searching expression on her face. If he stayed still for too long, though, Iteung would take both his hands and place them on her breasts. The good guy understood what she wanted and his hands would begin to move.

Once Iteung let out a moan, her voice like a dying cow, then it would be Good Budi's turn. Iteung would roll off him to the side, and now Good Budi could be on top. Good Budi didn't like any funny stuff, so he would assume the missionary position and get to work. Not long afterward he would kneel and ejaculate onto Iteung's stomach.

That's the only way this fight will be won, she thought to herself.

—

His body looked like it had been burned. When they looked at him, it was as if they could see the flames dance along the surface of his skin. His hands were clenched, as if he were enduring a blazing heat. Stripped to his underwear, but still dripping with sweat, he glared at the people around him, as if his eyes could devour whatever they saw. The two men stepped toward him, but then came the voice of the old blind man, not far from them.

"Let him be."

Ajo Kawir walked to the water trough, his hands still clenched into fists, his head still on fire. Then he plunged his head into the water and stayed there, even though his arms and legs began to twitch.

—

"Iteung! Wait, Iteung!" Iteung kept walking, while the guy hurried along behind her. "Iteung, tell me, is it true that you are with that hoodlum?"

"He's not a hoodlum and yes, I'm in love with him. He's my boyfriend."

"You slut! You're dumping me for that asshole?"

"What do you mean?"

"You're my girlfriend."

"You're not my boyfriend! We never said we were going out."

"So then what did it mean that you slept in my bed? Did it mean nothing that I had your pussy more than once?"

"You are not my boyfriend, and don't call him a hoodlum or an asshole, unless you want me to beat you up."

Good Budi watched Iteung walk away from him, her steps full of conviction. He didn't chase after her. He just stood there, his eyes welling up—he felt stabbed to the heart.

—

The two men were sitting in a small hall where visitors and inmates could meet. It wasn't the area for regular visitors, which was guarded by wardens and only open at certain hours. They were in the hall where special visitors could enter through a special door, even though they still had to get a stamp on their hand as if they were going to a theme park—and of course, they had to slip a bill into the guard's palm.

The room was a comfortable place to rest as the midday slowly turned into afternoon. Even though it didn't have any air conditioning, there was a large fan and it wasn't crowded at all—that afternoon, it was just the two of them. You could order coffee and refreshments from the canteen and sometimes there'd be the special prisoners, usually rich men or ex-officials, visiting with their families, who'd shower them with cartons and cartons of food.

A third man came in. He stood by the door and glared at the two men. It was Ajo Kawir.

"Why is he here?" one whispered. It made sense that he was uneasy. They were both right to worry. Ajo Kawir should not have been there.

—

In those days she always had an urge to go see Good Budi. Dammit, she thought, why did that guy, who she actually didn't like at all, always reappear in her mind on days like this? She knew that she wanted him, but she knew that she shouldn't want him.

To quell her gloomy feelings, Iteung would go to the academy or to the soccer stadium and run on the track. She hadn't been a student at the Kalimasada Silat Academy for a long time, but she knew the teachers and students and they'd let her come use their facilities. Running around the soccer field was the most effective way to kill her gloom. She was a good runner, and once she had started her run she never stopped, never allowing her legs to rest for even a moment—not even slowing to walk—until it was time to stop.

Her gloomy mood would return as soon as she stopped running and took a rest. When this mood came, the thoughts of throwing herself into Good Budi's embrace always appeared. The damn thing was, Good Budi was always there. He was always there whenever she was feeling blue.

"I know you love him," Good Budi said. "Even though maybe he's already forgotten all about you."

Her eyes welled up. Maybe she was remembering the last time she saw him, in front of that grocery store, when she had stood there in the rain and he had refused her love. She felt even more melancholy. When Good Budi took her hand, she didn't respond. When Good Budi embraced her, she didn't react. But she really did need someone to hold her.

"I will always love you, always long for you, always desire you."

Iteung almost didn't hear what Good Budi was saying. She fell into his arms, before she realized what she was doing and pulled away, aghast. Good Budi wanted to embrace her again, but she had already slipped out of his grasp. Then she stood and walked away. No, she thought. This must not happen.

—

Ajo Kawir walked toward them. They were still both sitting on a long bench, smoking. They were allowed to smoke there. There was concern on their faces. It wasn't an easy matter to face Ajo Kawir if there were only two of them. Of course, they had been able to subdue him thus far but usually with the old blind man by their side, and a warden, and sometimes a few others. But now it was only the two of them, and Ajo Kawir was walking closer with a fierce look in his eye.

Once Ajo Kawir reached them, he immediately sat down right between them. This wasn't going to be easy, they thought. It would not be easy to face someone who'd had the balls to kill the Tiger.

—

Despite his overflowing enthusiasm when he was in bed naked, there were a lot of annoying things about Good Budi. For one thing, he was whiny. Not many people knew that he was whiny, but Iteung knew. Truly whiny—a real crybaby. And that afternoon, for the umpteenth time, Iteung saw him cry.

"I'm begging you, Iteung, don't marry him!"

"I will marry him. I love him and he loves me."

Good Budi didn't even try to wipe his tears away. And maybe that was one of the good things about him: he wasn't too proud to get all weepy in front of Iteung. After falling silent and looking at each other for a few moments, without shame Good Budi said: "At least, make love to me, Iteung. For the last time. I want you."

"No."

—

This time he didn't cry. He was like a true friend who'd always be there for her. Like an old boyfriend who was waiting faithfully.

"You're not happy in your marriage, Iteung."

"I am happy."

"Don't lie. I can see it. I can feel it."

Good Budi tried to take Iteung's hand, but Iteung had already pulled it away. Good Budi did not force it any further. He knew that if he pushed the limits, Iteung would attack him and leave him lying black and blue in a ditch.

—

The room suddenly felt ice cold. Neither man dared look at Ajo Kawir. The old blind man failed us, they thought, and now he's going to get his revenge for all those nights he was whipped and beaten and drowned—its just a matter of time before a brutal fight breaks out in this room.

"No, I'm not going to attack you," Ajo Kawir suddenly spoke. "The fire of my rage is already out. It's sleeping soundly, just like my little bird."

—

Iteung always wished that some miracle would make her husband's pecker wake up. She'd try to wake it up, but then would let her husband's hand slide down between her legs, where she was already wet. She would close her eyes and, who knows why, she would imagine Mr. Toto's jet-black cock. She couldn't get rid of that image. Even after she let out a long moan.

—

"You're not happy in your marriage, Iteung." She didn't say anything. She didn't say anything when Good Budi took her hand. She didn't do anything when Good Budi began to embrace her. She didn't do anything when Good Budi moved his face closer to her and kissed her cheek. She didn't do anything when he kissed her lips.

She knew her body needed more than just clever dancing fingers. She imagined Mr. Toto's dark genitals, but this time with a feeling of disgust. She would never have them. But she could have Good Budi's privates. She'd had them before, and was sure she could have them again. All she had to do was do nothing.

Iteung didn't do anything when Good Budi began to undress her. She didn't do anything when he laid her down. But when he threw himself on top of her, Iteung began to move. She held him in between her thighs. She wriggled and squirmed. She closed her eyes and imagined she was lying underneath her husband.

❊ 7 ❊

"I CAN FIND those two policemen," said Uncle Bunny. "I know that they're really asshole crooks. You can send them to Krakatoa Crater. I can help."

"Thank you. But there's no use—let them be."

"But maybe that could make your ... thingy ..."

"Wake up?" Ajo Kawir pulled down his pants right in front of Uncle Bunny, pushing down his underwear too, and asked, "Bird, do you want to wake up? Uncle Bunny is inviting you to come out and play. Maybe he wants to promote you—make you a Military Commander." Then he looked up at Uncle Bunny: "Did you hear that? He says he wants to keep sleeping."

—

"Can I join you? I don't want to inconvenience you. I can pay my own way, buy all my own meals. I just need a ride."

"Well, we should ask my little bird," said Ajo Kawir.

Jelita peeked down at the truck driver's pants, and then after falling silent for a moment, she stooped down.

"Hey, what do you think you're doing?"

"Me? Well I'm going to open your fly. I want to ask your—"

"Oh, goddammit. He doesn't want to talk to you."

—

Eleven minutes in and Gaptooth Mono still hadn't found a way to win the fight. The truck drivers had threatened him before it all began that if he ran away from the fight, he would be ordered to screw a dog in front of all of them, or he would get buttfucked by male dogs in heat. And Gaptooth Mono knew the drivers weren't joking around.

The truck drivers had their own way of solving any problems that arose amongst them. They'd already agreed that the business between Gaptooth Mono and the Beetle had to be settled at the rubber plantation's fighting arena. The Beetle would not be allowed to ram anything up Gaptooth Mono's asshole—not his dick, not anything. Gaptooth Mono wouldn't have to replace the ruined Marilyn Monroe truck. But they had to fight to settle things, and the truck drivers would bet on who'd win.

—

Gaptooth Mono had always wished he could walk through a crowd and people would shy away from him in fear. Maybe this fight would be his chance, his only chance, to let everyone know that he was a tough guy.

"If I'm able to become a real tough guy," he once said, "then I won't be ashamed to go back to my village and see her."

—

They would face each other in the pigfighting arena. Sometimes cockfights were held there too, but a fight of man against man, with blood spraying everywhere, maybe even with shredded flesh and broken bones sticking out, brought in even more spectators than a pack of wild dogs swarming a pig, or tough cocks cutting each other up with spurs.

Those competitions were put on by a group of soldiers who informally owned the arena. Not many knew where they got the fighters, but the old hands among the gamblers would say, "The soldiers bring them from Aceh, or Papua, or Ambon—anywhere where there's a military operation."

Gossip had it that the soldiers sometimes took rebels or rioters who had surrendered and repented. Even if they were sure that these people were truly reformed, they'd still take them to the arena and order them to fight.

"Prove that you love Indonesia," whoever had captured them would say. "These maniac gamblers need some entertainment, and I'm sure you need some cash."

Thus, an ex-soldier from the Free Papua movement might fight with a Darul Islam sympathizer, and a Republic of South Maluku activist might spar with a Malacca Strait pirate. They would pit an East Timorese guerilla against an ex-communist they'd taken out of Salemba prison.

—

Of course, these fights didn't end just when a leg broke or an eyeball was plucked out and flung into a stray kitten's mouth. Only if one of the fighters was really in a bad way would the person who'd brought him throw in the towel, ending the fight. The loser would be insulted and abused—pelted with half-eaten snake fruit and water bottles. But losing fighters could recover, practice harder, and then probably get tossed into the pig-fighting ring again with a different opponent, or the same opponent, a few months after his loss. And people would bet on him again.

The truck drivers loved watching these fights and sometimes they spent all their money betting. But this kind of entertainment didn't happen that often, even with the turmoil that never stops in the far-flung corners of this republic—so now they were coming with fighters from their own ranks. The soldiers had no problem with it, because of course they always got a cut, no matter who was fighting.

—

"You know I'm in the middle of washing up, why did you burst in all of a sudden? Get out, you little creep!" Ajo Kawir pushed Gaptooth Mono back out, though at first the kid tried to stay in.

"It's your own fault. Why don't you lock the door?"

"Bullshit. You knew there was someone inside—and you know there's no lock."

"Of course I know, but … I wanted to ask your dick if I really have to fight the Beetle or not?"

"What?"

"I want to ask your dick."

"You jerk. Go ask the devil."

"But you're always asking your penis questions."

"That's my private business. Dammit."

—

He was reminded of his fight with the Tiger, which of course wasn't really a fight. Gaptooth Mono would lose, he was sure of that.

"Can't we just run away?" Gaptooth Mono asked him.

"We could," Ajo Kawir replied. "Somewhere far away. Maybe

Manado, or Ternate. I think the truck drivers would never find us someplace like that. I don't know exactly where those cities are, but they're really far away."

"But if I have the guts to fight him—and maybe if I can even defeat him—he'll stop trying to get up inside my ass."

That was true. Ajo Kawir knew it was true. But the problem was, the kid was no match for the Beetle, who'd happily pulverize him, even kill him. But he knew that Gaptooth Mono wasn't The Beetle's ultimate goal.

"So, you're going to prove that you're a real tough guy?"

———

"Why do you want to be a truck driver?" Ajo Kawir asked, while looking the kid over. He had previously had a *kenek* who was an old man he'd met in prison, who'd introduced him to the life of a truck driver. But after a few months, the old man's child asked him to come home and after Ajo Kawir spent a few days looking for a new *kenek*, the old man reappeared and offered him the kid.

"I want to become a tough guy."

Ajo Kawir was silent for a moment. "A truck driver isn't a tough guy."

"Fine, I don't care. But it seems like a truck driver's life is filled with adventures, a lot of excitement, a lot of insults, and fighting. What other job gives you such opportunity to become truly tough?"

"Okay, Tough Guy."

In fact, he had just run away from home, from his village. And to become a *kenek* and a relief truck driver was the first job he could find. In any case, he had driven the truck that belonged to his friend's father, the copra facility overseer.

———

The arena was deep inside the rubber plantation, a few kilometers from the border between West and Central Java, and there wasn't even really a village nearby, nothing but the plantation office, a few scattered houses, a food stall, an auto shop, and a school.

If someone was badly injured, there was no health clinic or hospital, no way they could get help fast—two men had died because of this. Their deaths were reported as resulting from a fight, with no mention that the fight had been organized by an underground gambling ring and bet on. The fighters knew the risks beforehand, knew they'd get a share of the gamblers' money.

But for Gaptooth Mono, this wasn't a question of money. This was a matter—just like when he'd lost his two front teeth—of becoming a tough guy.

—

"Bet all my money on the Beetle," Gaptooth Mono said to Ajo Kawir.

"What are you talking about? You might lose, but you should never *plan* to lose."

"Well in this case, if I lose, at the very least I'll get a lot of money."

"And what if you die?"

"Give the money to Nina, the girl in the photo."

The fight was about to start. People were already gathered around the bamboo fence lining an elevated platform: it was designed for pig and dog fights, which made it impossible for a fighter to escape from the arena.

From a diesel generator running at a distance, a cable stretched to two spotlights illuminating the arena—their light only made the darkness around it seem all the more impenetrable. Nothing beyond was visible but the shadows of people moving back and forth, flickering flames from lighters, and the glowing tips of cigarettes.

Only a few policemen or soldiers—at that time they weren't all that different, both were part of the Armed Forces—were allowed to use flashlights, and they rarely turned them on.

Someone whispered: "Here comes the Beetle—he looks ready to get started."

—

He was eating with the woman in a roadside food stall. Jelita. Gaptooth Mono was sleeping in the truck cabin. Another truck had just stopped and the *kenek* climbed down and approached their table. He looked to be in his fifties and walked with a slight limp.

"I have a message from the Beetle."

"What does he want?"

"You can save the kid—you can take his place. The Beetle wants to fight you."

"Tell the Beetle that I don't fight anyone anymore."

"The Beetle says that you'll eventually fight again."

"My bird says that I'm not allowed to fight."

People didn't know that his penis couldn't stand up, but they'd often heard that Ajo Kawir consulted it in all matters.

—

"Why do you always ask your pecker about everything?" Gaptooth Mono asked once, curious.

"All of human existence is nothing but a dream our genitals are dreaming. We're just here to act it out."

Gecko would have said that was philosophy.

—

"I want to help you," said Uncle Bunny. "Because, directly or indirectly, I'm the one who made you unable to get an erection."

"And how could that be possible?"

"It's entirely possible. If I had protected Agus Cornpipe, he wouldn't have died. If he hadn't died, Scarlet Blush wouldn't have gone crazy. If she hadn't gone crazy, the two policemen wouldn't have raped her, and if those two policemen hadn't raped her, you guys wouldn't have been at the house that night. And if you hadn't been there at the house that night, you would still be able to get an erection."

"That's nonsense. It was just a coincidence. It just so happened, that night, the Bird decided to go beddy-bye. In fact, if anyone is to blame, it's Nini Jumi."

"Who's Nini Jumi? What did she do?"

"Nini Jumi is a masseuse. If she hadn't tripped that day behind her house, she would have gone out to give a massage, and if she had given a massage, Mah Roah's sore neck would have healed, and if Mah Roah hadn't had a sore neck, she would have gone to the market, and if she had gone, she would have met a scruffy cat named Roma Irama. If—"

"Okay, stop. Listen, kid, I really want to help you."

"I'm not a kid anymore. You already sent a doctor to jail to examine me, and he couldn't find anything wrong. Take it easy, Uncle. The Bird is doing just fine. He told me he's dreaming about eating barley that tastes like roast beef."

"Well, it's up to you. But keep these, in case you change your mind."

Uncle Bunny—who was getting old, even though he still liked to wear those clothes that Ajo Kawir found so pathetic—held out two photographs, before leaving the truck depot with his driver.

—

The kid was curled up in the truck cabin, sobbing. Ajo Kawir ordered him to open the door to the cabin, locked from inside, but the kid didn't budge. A light drizzle was falling. Ajo Kawir pounded on the door, the kid still didn't get up, and he screamed, you dummy, open the door! The kid stayed curled up, crying his heart out as the drizzle started turning into a heavier rain. Ajo Kawir and Jelita were forced to take shelter under the awning of a closed food stall.

After about half an hour, when the rain had stopped, the kid finally opened the door, maybe because he was hungry.

"Dammit, why are you being such a crybaby? Are you afraid to fight the Beetle?"

The kid didn't admit it or deny it. He only remarked, "They say the Beetle actually wants to fight you."

"That's true. So you don't want to fight him anymore? If not, let's leave right now. We'll stop driving this truck."

"You don't want to fight him?"

"No. I already said, I'm leading a peaceful life just like—"

"I miss her."

"What?"

"I miss Nina." He began to cry again. Tears streamed down his face. Ajo Kawir and Jelita just looked at each other, not knowing how to stop the kid from being such a sap over a girl they didn't even know.

—

Hidden only by a mahogany tree, they stood by the roadside with their pants pulled halfway down their asses and their piss gushing onto its trunk. Piss is the most refreshing beverage for trees, Ajo Kawir said. And shit that's buried in the dirt, said Gaptooth Mono, is delicious food for their roots.

"Listen, big brother," said Gaptooth Mono. This was the first time the kid had ever called Ajo Kawir "big brother," so, still peeing on the mahogany tree, he listened closely. "I've already braced myself. I'm not afraid to lose to the Beetle—I'm not even afraid to die. Remember, I'm going to be a tough guy. I'm only afraid of one thing. I'm afraid I'm never going to see Nina again."

"You don't have much time. If you die in that fight, you'll never get to see her, except maybe in hell."

"Look at my wee-wee, big brother. It's good. My friends all told me it's good—it's big, it's long, it's dark, and when it's erect, it's as hard as the handle of a scythe. And I swore that I'd never use it with anyone except with Nina."

"What? So you've never used it with a woman before?"

"Never."

"Oh for the love of God!"

—

Someone adjusted one of the spotlights so that its beam fell fully on the right side of the arena, while the other spotlight illuminated the left side. The Beetle stood right smack in the middle of the circle, looking impatient under the bright lights.

A small door in one corner opened. Less than a meter tall, it was usually where the pigs or dogs came out, and there the kid was pushed out into the arena. He slipped and fell to loud jeers from the crowd, but all he could see were heads in the shadows. The kid clumsily rushed to stand up.

Ajo Kawir stood clutching the bamboo fence when suddenly a freezing cold hand grabbed his and held it tightly.

He looked over. That woman, Jelita, squeezed his hand tighter, giving him a penetrating chill.

"The kid won't survive."

—

Gaptooth Mono remembered looking at Nina in the dim light and scattered drizzle of the outdoor movie screening. Nina was sitting on a long bench that belonged to a boiled-peanut seller. Two guys were sitting on her left and right, and another was standing behind her. They couldn't have been more than eighteen or nineteen years old. The four of them were talking about something, and laughing. Even from where he was sitting, Gaptooth Mono could discern Nina's laughter and it made his heart pound like crazy.

The kid standing behind Nina wrapped his arm around her neck—she nudged him and told him to get off. The guys just laughed but Nina nudged him again, and the kid removed his arm.

Then the kid on her right-hand side put his left hand in Nina's lap, pawing at the girl's thigh. Nina pushed the kid to get him off her, grabbed his hand and removed it from her lap.

In the dim light, Gaptooth Mono could see it all. He felt his blood boil.

"My Nina," he muttered under his breath.

—

In his head, he imagined himself walking toward the peanut seller's bench. And like Clark Kent ... Wait, no. He preferred to imagine himself as Sylvester Stallone. Wait, not him either. Stallone looked too white, and went a little overboard, he was too cheesy. What about Barry Prima, Indonesia's Bruce Lee? He looked a little like a white guy, but also kind of like a Goody Two-shoes. Maybe Advent Bangun was better: before he was an actor he'd been a karate champ and he was intimidating, he was tough. Gaptooth liked that. Or how about if he was Maman Robot, the terrifying market thug? But finally he decided to just be himself—but the version of himself that existed in his mind, of course.

He would walk over to the peanut seller's bench with confident strides. He wished that he was a little taller and that his muscles were two times bigger and firmer, but he would stand in front of Nina and the three guys.

"Leave the young lady alone," he'd say, glaring at the three teens. Uh-oh, his voice didn't sound bold enough. He had to change it. "You jerks, leave this girl alone."

Of course, the three young men wouldn't stand for such an affront. Even though Gaptooth Mono looked intimidating, they outnumbered him. All three would stand, their hands curling into fists.

"Who are you, you bastard?" one of them would bark.

Gaptooth Mono would yell back, even louder, exactly a quarter inch in front of the guy's nose, "I'm Gaptooth Mono, you pig!"

"Stop! Stop!" Nina would try to break it up.

But they didn't want to stop. The kid who'd just been screaming at Gaptooth Mono, getting right in his face, would be spattered by some of Gaptooth Mono's spit, and even more pissed off, he'd advance, grabbing a fistful of Gaptooth Mono's collar and shoving him. One of the other guys would punch Gaptooth Mono in the stomach—*oof!* Gaptooth Mono would fly backward, letting out a grunt, and the last guy would punch him in the head.

Now Gaptooth Mono would have a million reasons to become savage and brutal. He would stare the three guys down and with an uncannily calm demeanor, he'd take off his shirt and throw it on the grass. In the light of the gas and oil lamps, people would see the big tattoos on his chest and back.

No, Gaptooth Mono didn't really have any tattoos. But in his imagination, at that point there'd be big tattoos. On his back there'd be a tiger crouching, Japanese yakuza-style, like ones he'd seen in movies. On his left pectoral, not too big, there'd be a dragon with fire shooting out of its mouth.

At the sight of all that, the three guys would choke. Gaptooth Mono would then put up his fists, looking just like Bruce Lee. They'd still be gasping as he hurled a punch at the guy who'd yelled at him. One punch, speeding right toward his mouth—*bam!* The kid's head would snap to the side, one tooth would go flying away on a spray of blood, but Gaptooth Mono wouldn't stop, throwing two more punches, three, four, until the kid fell sprawling onto the grass, smeared with blood.

The kid would try to stand up and run away, but Gaptooth Mono wouldn't be finished yet. He'd tackle him, twisting the kid's arm. You'd hear the kid begging, I give up! Have mercy! *Bam! Bam! Bam!* Gaptooth Mono would throw more punches until the kid's nose looked like it had caved in.

The two friends would turn pale at all of this and quickly vanish. Calmly, stretching and shaking out his fingers, Gaptooth Mono would look over at Nina. "Are you all right, my darling?"

—

In actuality, he just stood rooted in place. And he was forced to watch the guy who was standing behind Nina again wrap his arm around the girl's neck, and then slide his hand down to fondle her breast. The girl squirmed, pushed the kid, stood up, and walked away, sulking. They laughed and hurried after her.

Gaptooth Mono felt the power drain out of his body. I should have, he thought. I should have gone over there and punched out all of them.

He should have studied martial arts so that he could do it easily. He should have been a frightening tough guy who'd make those three guys piss their pants and go running off, just by appearing. He should have a bigger, stronger body—he should have an invincible body, impervious to all weapons, so that he could protect the girl he loved, taking them down should be easy for him, so all he'd have to do was grab one guy's wrists and twist. He should be able to kick their knees and break them in half. He should …

All those thoughts made his head throb.

———

The Beetle lunged at him, throwing a punch, but with his small body, Gaptooth Mono was able to jump back, dodging to the side. Furious, the Beetle swung his fist once again. The blow grazed Gaptooth Mono's temple, but once again he was able to jump to the side and avoid getting slammed. The Beetle chased him, but Gaptooth Mono kept his distance.

"Cut it out, you monkey!" yelled the Beetle. His eyes, red with fury, bulged out and caught the spotlight's beam.

Gaptooth Mono didn't say anything. At this point, he hadn't thrown any punches of his own, and he still didn't—glimpsing a fist whirring past his nose, he just kept on jumping to the side.

———

She had never seen such a calm man. Still gripping his hand tightly, she peered over at him again and again, studying the expression on his face. Ajo Kawir didn't respond, just kept looking into the arena dispassionately, as if nothing important was going on there.

"If you can't stomach watching them fight, then leave," he said. "Wait beside the ticket booth."

Jelita didn't say anything—she wanted to leave, but she was worried about the kid, who was still dancing around, dodging sometimes to the left and sometimes to the right, avoiding the Beetle as people began to shout in annoyance, because they still hadn't seen a real fight.

—

Gaptooth Mono waited under the sawo tree at the bend in the road. He knew that at this time of day Nina would appear, coming home from her job at a clothing store in front of the market. He pretended he was seeking shade, on an afternoon that was in fact already overcast, leaning against the tree trunk, nervously clutching a cigarette. And finally Nina did appear.

"Mono, what are you up to over there?"

"Who, me? Just resting on my way back from the copra plant, washing the trucks. You're on your way home?"

"Yup."

They had been friends and neighbors for a long time—practically the same age—but friendship wasn't really what Gaptooth Mono wanted. He wanted more. He'd fallen in love with Nina.

So as they walked side by side, Gaptooth Mono couldn't help stealing glances at her skin, her soft hair, the swell of her breasts and the curve of her lips. He wanted to take her hand, he wanted everything.

"Nina …"

A muddy Jeep drove up and stopped right beside them. The driver's side window rolled down, revealing a man looking over at them. He smiled.

"Nina, I went looking for you at your house but you weren't there. Come for a ride with me."

"But, Brother …"

"It's okay. I already got your mother's permission. Come on, let's go."

Nina looked over at Gaptooth Mono, and then opened the door and climbed in. Gaptooth Mono didn't have the chance to open his mouth—the Jeep pulled away, just like that, leaving behind a cloud of exhaust smoke as if it had farted in his face.

All Gaptooth Mono could do was swallow his rage. And when he couldn't take it any more, he swore: "Bastard!"

—

When he tried to avoid the next punch, his left foot stumbled over his right, and he lost his balance. Gaptooth Mono tripped and fell, and when he tried to get up again, the Beetle was looming over him.

Gaptooth Mono flailed, trying to grab the Beetle's arm. But his opponent wasn't stupid, and he moved to quickly seize his arm and bent it back, while his other hand pounded Gaptooth's nose. The kid screamed.

Gaptooth Mono tried to wriggle free but the Beetle kept on hurling punches. Another one hit the kid's nose. *Bam!*

—

"The kid's going to die. He's going to die. The Beetle is going to kill him. He's going to die. The Beetle is going to kill him just to make you mad."

Jelita was clutching Ajo Kawir's hand but Ajo Kawir still wasn't responding, just looking straight ahead at Gaptooth Mono, who was trying to escape the Beetle's attack. The kid's face was already red, smeared with his own blood.

"You have to stop him—you have to save the kid," Jelita said.

—

Out back behind his house, Gaptooth Mono sat at the edge of the banana orchard. His chest was bare, and he'd hung his shirt on the clothesline. Afternoon was turning into evening. He looked at his biceps, his chest, his stomach. He hated his body. If he had a bigger, more muscular body, maybe he would have been able to yank that bastard out of his Jeep and beat him up in the roadside. Or maybe if he was a rich man's son, and had a nice car, or if he …

He could feel his head throbbing steadily. He almost didn't realize that Ujang, one of his friends from the copra plant, was approaching.

"Daydreaming?" asked Ujang. "Pining for Nina?"

"Shut up, asshole."

"I already told you that if you get some money, you can have Nina. At least for a night."

Actually, all his friends at the copra plant had told him that numerous times. He didn't believe it. But they did. His head throbbed even more insistently.

———

At one point, Gaptooth Mono got the chance to escape the Beetle's onslaught—the kid jumped back, then went off running around the perimeter of the arena, his enemy in hot pursuit.

The spectators broke out into an uproar: Water bottles started to fly, along with snakefruits, curses, and insults.

———

A few soldiers tried to calm the unruly crowd, barking at whoever was throwing drinks or pieces of fried cassava, but even while they approached one group of spectators, another group would do the same thing, and Gaptooth Mono was kept busy trying to fend off all the objects flying his way.

The Beetle didn't waste the opportunity and immediately went straight for Gaptooth Mono's knee—the kid didn't have the chance to dodge and a blow landed full force on his kneecap.

Crackkk!

Gaptooth Mono's leg bent backward. Now everyone heard the kid let out a bloodcurdling scream, swaying back and forth until he collapsed in the dirt. The Beetle didn't pay that scream any mind and leapt on top of him, his fists pummeling the kid's face.

The Beetle looked out toward the spectators and glared right where Ajo Kawir—returning his gaze—was standing.

—

"Don't you see? The kid's knee is ruined. You have to stop it. Now!" Jelita shook Ajo Kawir. "The Beetle wants to fight you. Save that kid, I'm begging you!"

Ajo Kawir looked down and asked, "Do you want to fight?" Then after a moment he looked back up at Jelita. "He said he still doesn't want to fight. He couldn't be bothered, he must be busy mulling something over."

"Your pecker can go to hell!"

—

His whole face was swollen, and he couldn't feel anything anymore. The pain in his knee, which he was sure was broken, was intolerable—no way he could stand. One more blow came whizzing and hit his temple. He was numb, but he knew the skin had split.

Half closed because of his swollen flesh, his eyes peered out at the crowd. He was searching, wondering whether Ajo Kawir would come to his aid. The Beetle wouldn't stop his assault unless he surrendered. But he wouldn't surrender, not unless that man watching waved his hand, stopping the fight—he wanted to be a tough guy. But the man gave no sign of stopping the fight. So there was nobody to intervene.

"Give up, kid," he heard the Beetle say.

"Why, you can't fight anymore? Have I worn you out?"

Bam! Another blow slammed him and there was another spray of blood.

—

It was getting near dawn and they were still fighting over the rest of the money in the card game pot at the village security post. All four kids worked at the copra plant and one of them, Marwan, had managed to empty out his three friends' pockets, but he hadn't ended the game—he was trying to see if he could truly bankrupt them.

"I need it to buy something sweet." Marwan said. "To pay Nina to sleep with me."

"That's bullshit. Nina would never be with you," said Ujang.

Gaptooth Mono stayed quiet. He was busy thinking how to win and get his money back from Marwan—that was the only way to make sure that Marwan wouldn't be able to go see Nina. Who knew whether what they said was true, that anyone could have the girl if they paid her?

The smell of charring coconut wafted from the copra plant; the smoke drifted in the air, mingling with the morning mist. A truck stopped and Gaptooth Mono got out, sulking, regretting that he'd gambled away all his money two nights ago, and now he couldn't buy even one single cigarette. He had to ask the old men at the copra plant for tobacco and a dried sugar palm leaf to roll his own.

When he walked past the coconut-stripping area, he saw Ujung and Marwan sitting on a big rock in the middle of the yard, drinking coffee. "So, did you get a little taste? How was it?"

"I sure did! Nina's crazy delicious—way better than using my hand. A month ago I got a blister from using laundry soap as lube."

Gaptooth Mono was positive they were saying that just to rile him up. He was certain that Nina wasn't like that. There was no money in the world that could buy her.

—

"Don't talk shit about Nina!" Gaptooth Mono stood in front of Marwan, snapping. "If you say anything else about her, I'll knock your teeth out!"

"You better not mouth off—you've already lost two teeth, how many more do you want to lose?" Marwan got heated and stood up. "What business do you have with Nina anyway?"

"Don't even say her name with your foul mouth."

"Nina. Nina. Nina! I slept with Nina. She's expensive but her hole's delicious, crazy."

Gaptooth Mono's fist flew into Marwan's face. Maran fell backward but quickly stood up again, holding his cheek. He advanced and threw his own punch, but Gaptooth Mono swiftly dodged, retaliating with another hit, this time to Marwan's mouth, knocking out one of his teeth—thick blood dripped from his gums.

Gaptooth Mono didn't want to stop. One more punch made three more of Marwan's teeth fly.

—

Ujang laughed. Marwan laughed. Then Marwan gave Ujang's arm a little jab, saying, "But take my advice—don't ever give Nina your money. You'll regret it."

"Why?"

"Because once you do it with her you'll want her again and again and again. You'll go broke!"

Ujang laughed, Marwan laughed, and this time Ujang jabbed Marwan's arm.

Gaptooth Mono should have barked at them: "Don't talk about Nina like that!" He should have punched Marwan in the mouth. Sent his teeth flying. But Gaptooth Mono was still just standing nearby, looking at his two friends. His head was getting hot.

He felt it throbbing, turned around and walked away.

—

After one more punch, the Beetle again looked in Ajo Kawir's direction as if to say, "Come down here, or I'll kill this kid right where he lies. I want to fight you." But Ajo Kawir didn't appear at all concerned.

Meanwhile, Gaptooth Mono, even though his eyes were almost swollen shut, saw his chance to escape, but he couldn't move his ruined right leg. Even so, he still had some energy, which he'd been preserving since the beginning of their fight, and he didn't want to waste this one tiny opportunity. He wriggled his torso, pushing the Beetle aside. Caught off guard, the Beetle lost his balance, and in that instant Gaptooth Mono pulled back his left leg and forcefully kicked the Beetle in the chin.

With a dislocated jaw, the Beetle bounced back, unable to close his mouth, letting out a long howl, and then falling into the dirt, flat as a pancake.

With his bruised face, Gaptooth Mono stood and tried to smile. He could only stand on one leg, but he did it, and took off the shirt he was wearing, rolled it up, and bit it. Then, closing his eyes, he grabbed hold of his right shin and, pulling it as hard as he could, reset the bone to the kneecap. He bit his shirt harder, and tears poured out. The bone was not set perfectly.

The spectators fell silent, witnessing the scene. The only sounds were the Beetle's angry grunts.

The Beetle stood up, his mouth hanging agape, just as Gaptooth Mono had reset his right shinbone—his leg still hurt like crazy, but it was way better than not being able to use it at all.

Now they were facing off once again. You could hear a pin drop.

The Beetle charged Gaptooth, full of rage, but Gaptooth no longer dodged him; instead he blocked blows and twisted the Beetle's arms, and with the Beetle stooped over, he raised his left knee to smash the man's face. *Bam!* Now it was the Beetle's blood splattering.

Gaptooth Mono seized the moment. Holding on to the Beetle, he thrust himself upward, flying into the air, and then with the help of his body weight, body-slammed the Beetle to the ground. The Beetle's head pounded against the grassy dirt. For a long time, his blood pooling around him, the Beetle didn't budge. When he could finally move, all he did was pat the ground three times. He surrendered.

The crowed roared. But Gaptooth's head was still throbbing insistently—he kept trouncing the Beetle, jamming two of his fingers right into the Beetle's eyeballs, plunging deep into his eye sockets. The Beetle howled and groped around blindly. He was about to crack the Beetle's neck when a soldier jumped into the arena and dragged him away.

"Stop, kid, unless you want to go to jail."

The Beetle might die, with a destroyed face to boot, if they didn't get him to the hospital immediately—it was fifty-five kilometers away.

———

"Tell me the secret of how to beat the Beetle," Gaptooth Mono said. "I'm sure you know—I've heard the other truckers say that you're a champion fighter. You killed the Tiger. Tell me the secret. The fighters' secret."

Ajo Kawir looked at him for a long time, with a reluctant expression.

———

The sales clerks in the market stores and kiosks were beginning to close up shop. Nina was just about to pull the last wooden slat closed when Gaptooth Mono appeared and gently pushed Nina back inside her shop, blocking the door.

"Nina, is it true that people can pay to sleep with you?"

Nina was taken aback and looked at Gaptooth Mono for a few moments before opening her mouth:

"You have some money? When you have some money, find a room and let me know."

When he heard that, Gaptooth Mono wanted to cry.

———

He cursed Marwan, who'd cleaned him out at cards—without money he couldn't rent a room or Nina.

Pissed off, he muttered, "Whore." And at that moment he noticed his mother's bedroom door ajar. He peeked in. The house was quiet and empty. He knew his parents, simple farmers, didn't have very much money. But he also knew that his mother saved a little bit of cash inside her clothes closet. He had never touched that money, but today would be the exception.

He walked slowly toward the bedroom door.

—

Nina sat on the edge of the bed. Gaptooth Mono took out all the money that he'd found in his mother's drawer and put it on top of the bedside table, reserving the amount it would cost to rent the room.

"That's all you have?"

"Mmmm…." Gaptooth Mono didn't know how much he was supposed to pay her. "I can give you more next month."

At first Nina didn't reply but then she said, "That's OK, this is enough."

Nina approached and squatted in front of him. Gaptooth Mono got goose bumps and his legs felt shaky. Nina unzipped his fly, and the kid felt even more goose bumps—the bird in his pants was getting big and hard, he knew it. Nina pulled down his pants.

"Your thing is good. Dark, big, hard."

Gaptooth Mono squeezed his eyes shut, trembling. Nina touched him, stroked him. Gaptooth Mono bit his lip. Nina kept on stroking him. Something urgently wanted to come out—one more touch, and that something gushed from the tip of Gaptooth Mono's cock.

"Oh, for heaven's sake, Mono!" Nina shrieked, and then burst out laughing. "I barely even touch it and you blow your load? You're a one-pump chump!" She kept on laughing, and Gaptooth Mono wanted to die.

—

"You bastard child! You stole your mother's money just to shove it up a woman. You bastard!"

The villagers laughed to see Gaptooth Mono's mother scold him in their front yard. He really and truly wanted to die.

"You idiot! You dropped out of school and now you steal your mother's money to stick your thing in a woman. Why don't you just stick it in one of the ducks out back behind the house? You could do all of them—for free! You bastard! You jerk! You fool! You asshole! You pig!"

After this, Gaptooth Mono vowed to run away from the village.

❈{ 8 }❈

"IF I HAD known that the Tiger was half-crippled like that, I never would've told you to kill him," Uncle Bunny said. He looked at Ajo Kawir with regret, which—to Ajo Kawir—made him look like a half-witted turtle.

"Don't get too worked up about it, Uncle. If I hadn't killed the Tiger that day, I would have killed somebody else. It made no difference to me."

Then Uncle Bunny asked whether he wanted to send anyone else to Krakatoa Crater. He told Ajo Kawir about a middle-aged woman who worked at the yarn factory—she was really a nuisance: first she had refused to work for one day, then two days, then a few days. The problem was, Uncle Bunny said, she had convinced more than a thousand other workers to join her on strike.

"You own that yarn factory, Uncle?"

"No. But that's not the issue. You want to know what the issue is?"

"No. And I have no desire to send her to Krakatoa Crater, Uncle. You know that."

"Yeah, I know. I just figured I'd ask."

—

A number of times he'd asked that woman who she was and where she was going. He could take her home, as long as she was willing to say where her home was.

"Who am I? I already told you, my name is Jelita. I don't want to tell you where I live. I ran away from home. I ran away from my husband. That's all you need to know."

The woman's name meant lovely, but whoever had given her that name, Ajo Kawir always thought, must have been making a big joke. She was ugly. He didn't need to dwell on what exactly her face looked like, but in Ajo Kawir's opinion, she was hideous. And he wasn't sure she was telling the truth. Ran away from her husband? Was there really a man on the face of this earth who'd have married a woman like this?

"Is it inconveniencing you, that I'm hitching a ride on your truck? If it's making trouble for you, I'll get off and look for another ride."

"No."

"Or do I have to pay you? With my money or my pussy?"

"No. No. You can hitch a ride in my truck. For free."

—

But there was something strange about this woman. He didn't speak about it with anyone. Not with Gaptooth Mono, and not even with Gecko. But clearly, there was something strange about her.

"Actually, you give off the impression that you don't need a woman. You're not like the other truck drivers. You never go to a whorehouse."

Ajo Kawir was taken aback, but regained his composure to say, "I have a wife."

"Mm-hmm."

Jelita had been his *kenek* for a number of days, even though she couldn't exactly be considered a real *kenek*. If there were a problem with the truck on the side of the road, Ajo Kawir would surely have to take care of it by himself. More precisely, she was simply always there, in Gaptooth Mono's seat, wherever the truck went. But no matter, he was happy that Jelita was keeping him company—it was better than having to navigate the roads all alone.

"How long do you think the kid'll have to stay in the hospital?"

"Maybe two weeks, and after that it'll take a few months for his broken leg to heal. Still, he'll probably limp for the rest of his life. I'm not sure he'll be able to work in this truck again."

"Is the hospital expensive?"

"Who knows? The soldiers are taking care of it. They're paying for his stay and will have to pay for his treatment."

He hadn't seen Gecko in a long time. It was always bittersweet to see him. Sometimes he visited him in Yogyakarta and sometimes Gecko met up with him at some truck depot. When they met, they'd always embrace, and take a good long look at each other.

That afternoon at the truck depot in Pluit, Gecko appeared. "I saw her, and she gave you a photo. A new photo."

Like always, Gecko handed him a photograph. It was a photo of the same young girl Ajo Kawir had stuck to his truck cabin ceiling. She'd gotten bigger. For the first time, there was something written on the back of the photograph. A little girl's handwriting: "Dad, when are you coming home? I want to see you. Grandma and Grandpa want to see you."

Ajo Kawir's eyes welled up.

———

"I heard that Uncle Bunny found those two policemen. Damn, it's so easy for them to find lowlifes like that. I think we have to kill them."

"No. I'm never going to kill anyone else ever again. My life has changed.... You know—"

"Yeah, I know. Your bird has taught you the way of tranquility. The path of peace."

They both were silent. Ajo Kawir was scrutinizing the photo for every new detail of the little girl's face, while Gecko was remembering their past, remembering a hellish night he still regretted at the house of Scarlet Blush.

"So tell me, who's that ugly woman with you? What? Her name is Jelita? You've got to be kidding me. Is she your woman, or a whore?"

"She's my *kenek*."

———

Gecko said he had to catch a train to Yogyakarta. Ajo Kawir wanted to take him to Gambir station in his truck. Don't be stupid, Gecko said. You could get arrested for taking a truck this big through the middle of the city. I'll go alone, I'll just take a taxi, but I have to hurry, I have to be back in Yogyakarta by morning. I have a business opportunity that I can't miss out on.

"All right," said Ajo Kawir. "But there's one more thing we need to talk about. When are you going to get married?"

This question made Gecko laugh. "I don't know. I never have any luck with women. I fall in love with someone who doesn't love me, or some woman likes me but she doesn't turn me on. Trust me, I'll tell you before sending out my wedding invitations."

Gecko had never told Ajo Kawir—he had never told anyone—that he had vowed to never touch a woman. He had vowed he would never put his dick in a woman until he knew that Ajo Kawir could get an erection. That was the only thing he could do to punish himself for all the foolish things he'd done in his early teenage years.

—

Ajo Kawir used to have wet dreams, of course, like other boys. But after what'd happened, after that crazy screwed up night, he'd never had another wet dream ever again. Not even when he *tried* to have one.

He occasionally found his pants wet in the morning, but he hadn't had a dream. They were just wet. Like a dam had been breached. At least once or twice a month. He never knew, when splooging in his sleep, whether the Bird had gotten big and hard or whether it had stayed flaccid, sleeping. All he knew was that his pants were wet, without dreaming.

But ever since Jelita had appeared, he had started to dream, dreams that ended with his underwear sticky.

There's something strange about that woman, he thought.

—

The woman was ugly, but when she took off her clothes, it was as if everything ugly about her vanished. Or rather, she was still ugly, but her ugliness seemed to excite him strangely.

They were sitting in the back of the truck, under a tarp, as rain poured down outside. The truck was practically empty except for the two of them, and Jelita's clothes, which were heaped in a corner along with a few other things. In the dim light of the small hanging emergency lamp, Ajo Kawir could see Jelita's naked body—ugly, but arousing.

Jelita unrolled the carpet where Gaptooth Mono usually slept and lay herself down there, looking seductively in Ajo Kawir's direction.

He approached her, and lay down beside her. Slowly, Jelita undid his fly, and, lowering her face, took hold of the Bird. Her mouth opened.

Ajo Kawir felt something urgently needing to come out, about to burst.

———

When he awoke, he found himself lying curled up on a bench at a gas station. The clock on the wall said it was past four in the morning. The gas station was quiet. There was only one other truck, whose driver was also resting. One attendant was stretched out on a couple of benches pushed together and the other one was filling in a crossword puzzle.

Jelita was also awake, sitting on the same bench where Ajo Kawir was curled up. She was reading a pulp novel that she had bought on the side of the road. Ajo Kawir looked over at her and Jelita returned his gaze. She smiled and Ajo Kawir felt embarrassed. Damn, he thought. Does she know I was dreaming about her—and not just dreaming about her, but having a *wet* dream about her? And this wasn't the first time.

"What?" asked Jelita, seeing the expression on his face.

"Nothing."

His underwear felt uncomfortable. It felt sticky. He had to hurry to the bathroom and wash the Bird.

———

The dawn call to prayer sounded softly. It was almost morning, he thought, what's the harm in bathing. At first he'd only intended to rinse off the Bird and change his underwear, but then he decided to bathe. He often washed up at gas stations. He liked their big bathrooms, with troughs overflowing with water. And he liked how they were always quiet.

In the bathroom, he saw that the Bird was indeed wet and sticky. Gecko had once said to him: "It doesn't matter that you don't use your bird, any healthy man produces a regular supply of jizz. Sooner or later, your balls will be full. You have to get the stuff out, no matter how, or else it will come out on its own, with dreams or not."

And now his had come out because of a dream. A dream about Jelita.

Ajo Kawir scooped up some water with the dipper, and as if he didn't want to think about his wet dream anymore, he poured it onto the crown of his head. He again doused himself, water was pouring down over his entire body—it felt cold in the frigid morning air, but also refreshing.

Suddenly he remembered something, realized something. He'd sensed it many times before, but only now did he truly realize it. The dream was crystal clear—and in the dream, the dream about lying down on the carpet in the truck next to Jelita, his bird had stood up, big and hard.

He bowed his head and asked, "Bird, did you wake up?"

There was no answer. Clearly, the Bird was still fast asleep. Ajo Kawir could practically hear it snoring.

—

Jelita sat in the passenger seat, wrapped in a blanket. Her head was tilted slightly to lean against the window, and her eyes were closed. She had fallen asleep as soon as she sat down and closed her eyes.

Ajo Kawir turned on the engine, and sat calmly behind the wheel. He wiped the windshield to get rid of the lingering morning dew. He waited a few moments until he thought the engine must be warm.

The bath had refreshed him. He was ready to drive the truck for a long way. Sitting there daydreaming, with his hands on the wheel, he once again remembered his strange dream about this strange woman.

He looked over. Snoring softly, Jelita appeared to be deeply asleep. Suddenly this thought appeared in Ajo Kawir's mind: "Do I have to sleep with this woman in order to prove that the Bird can get up like it did in my dream?"

He looked at Jelita for a long time. No, he thought. This woman doesn't turn me on at all. That was just a dream.

"You don't miss your wife?" Jelita asked. Ajo Kawir was startled. He hadn't noticed that the woman had woken up, and all of sudden she was asking him that question.

Feeling that there was no reason to lie, he said, "Of course I miss her."

"Why don't you go see her?"

This time, Ajo Kawir didn't know what to say. He was silent, and kept driving with his eyes looking straight ahead. Jelita seemed to be waiting for his response. Ajo Kawir stole a glance at her, and finally said:

"She's still in jail. And ... well, fine, the fact is I don't want to see her."

—

In addition to being dislocated, his kneecap was also cracked. That was why they sent him to the hospital, and not to Cimande where the bonesetter lived. The hospital gave him a cast for his leg, and

Gaptooth Mono had to convalesce in his hospital bed for a long time.

If they passed that way, Ajo Kawir and Jelita would stop and see the kid. They would bring him his favorite foods and martial arts comics.

"I heard that in a few days you're going to be discharged?"

"Yeah, that's what they said, and I don't have to pay for any of it, the soldiers are going to pay."

"Here are your earnings that you asked me to keep for you. You should go home to your village and rest." Ajo Kawir placed a brown paper envelope on the small table next to the hospital bed. "And here's some more money—you won the bet at the rubber plantation." Ajo Kawir put down another, even fatter, brown paper envelope.

"What bet?"

"I didn't do what you told me. I bet all your money that you'd win."

Reaching for the fatter brown envelope, the kid looked at Ajo Kawir in disbelief, opened it, and took out what was inside. Indeed, there was a pile of money and he knew it was a lot. If I use this to pay Nina, he thought, I could sleep with her for a couple of weeks straight, maybe even a couple of months.

The doctor had told him to begin to practice walking, using crutches, and Ajo Kawir kept him company as he walked, one leg swinging in its cast, around the hospital grounds.

"How's the Beetle?" he asked.

"They were able to save one of his eyes, but he can't see very well. He stopped driving trucks. He's probably mad at you, but in his condition, I don't think he'll come after you. He won't try to fight."

The kid laughed and kept walking.

"So tell me, you were so sure I was going to win the fight that you bet all my money on me?"

"No," Ajo Kawir said. "I bet on you because everybody else bet on the Beetle."

"You asshole!"

"Don't curse at me—now you have the money to go home."

Gaptooth Mono thought of Nina, how he missed her so much, and how much unfinished business he had with her.

—

"Tell me the secret of a real fighter, I'm begging you," said Gaptooth Mono, looking at Ajo Kawir with moist, pathetic eyes.

"I don't have any advice at all. I'm not sure you can win this fight. But ..."

"Say it. Say it, brother."

"This will be difficult. But if you get the opportunity, you should poke out his eyeballs. That's your only chance."

Gaptooth Mono fell silent. He knew that would be almost impossible.

—

That dream—that wet dream—came again, this time while he was napping behind the wheel. Exhausted, Ajo Kawir had decided to rest in front of a line of food stalls. Jelita could not really be called a *kenek*, since she didn't know the way and she didn't even know how to drive a truck, so Ajo Kawir had nobody to take his place when he got sleepy, and had to stop.

He woke up feeling more refreshed than he had in a long time. When he opened his eyes, he could still remember his dream vividly, but when he looked over and there was Jelita, reading her pulp novel, honestly he felt embarrassed again. He felt like he'd been caught in the act.

"What?" Jelita asked.

"Nothing. I'm just surprised that I fell asleep here."

Of course, Jelita knew he was lying. Falling asleep in the driver's seat was nothing out of the ordinary for truck drivers.

Damn, he thought. In that dream he found Jelita in a river. He was walking and he heard the sound of splashing water. Someone must be bathing in the river, he thought. He peeked through the leaves, and he was right, he saw a woman bathing.

Even in his dream, Jelita looked as ugly as she did in real life. Forget any man being aroused by looking at her, even a crocodile would be reluctant to make her his prey, thinking that maybe a gruesome djinn was taking a bath. But in dreams, something's always different from real life.

Ajo Kawir felt his body grow warm when he saw Jelita bathing, and at that moment his bird woke up. It didn't just wake up, it stretched as if it wanted to take flight. Ajo Kawir felt restless, just crouching there and spying.

"Older brother, why don't you join me in the river?" He heard Jelita calling him, "Come on!" and saw her flirtatious gaze aimed at the brush where he was lurking.

Ajo Kawir came out of his hiding place and now he could see the woman's body clearly, under the perfectly transparent water. "Come on in!" Jelita yelled. Hesitantly he took off his clothes and slowly walked into the water. His feet were wet. His thighs were wet. He went deeper and deeper into the water and when the river touched his pecker, the water felt warm. To him it felt like the clear water was an extension of Jelita's body, soft and smooth. The Bird writhed and squirmed and finally, spewed.

"Hey, what's wrong with your bird?"

"Sorry," Ajo Kawir said, embarrassed. "He has the flu."

—

"Who has the flu?" Jelita asked, pulling her eyes away from her pulp novel and looking over at Ajo Kawir.

"What?"

"You were talking in your sleep. And you said, sorry he has the flu. Who has the flu? You were dreaming."

There was no way he would tell her. *Damn*, he thought, feeling his cheeks turn red. He didn't dare look over but just shook his head and then opened the cabin door, got out of the truck, and went to the bathroom behind the row of food stalls.

—

While squatting on the toilet and getting rid of all the food he'd eaten over the past two days, Ajo Kawir decided to have a little chat with the Bird. He felt like the Bird was hiding something, and as the closest person to the Bird in the entire world, he felt slighted.

"We already promised that there would be no secrets between us," Ajo Kawir said, looking down at his crotch. He could see lumps of shit piled on top of each other in the toilet hole. He didn't care. He wasn't looking at the shit, he was looking at his Bird. "Tell me, what's going on with you?"

The Bird was still curled up, in the same exact position he had been in for years.

"I'm mad at you, Bird," Ajo Kawir said in annoyance.

Like I care, maybe that's what the Bird was thinking.

Ajo Kawir scooped some water out of the water trough with his dipper, and still feeling a little resentful, he poured it over the Bird. But the little lumps of shit were also splashed with water and splattered, jumping every which way. He was lucky none flew up into his face. Ajo Kawir got even more annoyed.

Stay calm, stay calm, he muttered. The Bird has already taught me how to stay calm. Don't get mad over a little bit of scattered shit. He closed his eyes and tried to relax.

"Be honest with me, Bird." He was still talking to the Bird, while drenching his body with water from the trough. "Did you wake up in my dream? Did you wake up and get big? Did you get hard?"

With an infuriatingly aloof demeanor, the Bird didn't respond.

"Don't tell me that your taste is really that bad, Bird? Don't tell me that you wake up for women that look like Jelita? I can find you something better."

You think women are just things, that you can buy at the Tanah Abang market?

"If it wasn't a dream, would you wake up, Bird? Would you get hard in front of Jelita in real life? Say something, Bird, because I really want to know."

—

If I can get an erection again, he thought, I will have a reason to go home. To see my little girl, and especially my wife. But after sleeping for years, maybe the Bird only wakes up for women like Jelita? And plus, that was only in a dream … but I've never dreamed about any other woman.

She is a strange woman. There's something strange in her. I only dream about this woman and no one else, and she gives me wet dreams. Don't tell me I have to ask her to sleep with me? But what if she's the only one who can make me hard?

"Are you daydreaming?" Jelita suddenly chided him. "Don't daydream while you're driving."

Ajo Kawir was startled, and then shook his head, not daring to look at her.

—

Gecko always brought up Iteung every time they met—including the last time, in the Pluit truck depot, when Gecko had given him the photograph of the little girl and said, "In no more than four weeks, she's going to get out of women's prison. You have to go home to greet her."

Ajo Kawir knew exactly when she was getting out of jail. The date was etched into his brain.

"Have you seen her often?"

"A few times. In fact, I'm the only one who is permitted to visit her, and you know why, because I already told you. She really misses you."

"I'm a useless husband."

"If you go home to greet her, you will be useful," Gecko said, right before he got into the taxi that would take him to Gambir Station.

—

He returned to thinking, if I could get hard, I could make Iteung happy. And I would also be happy. And maybe even just one day of shared happiness could erase all these years of suffering. But is sleeping with Jelita the only way to make my Bird wake up, as my dreams suggest?

"Your mind is wandering again," Jelita scolded him.

"I'm sorry," Ajo Kawir finally said, and this time he looked over. "You said you ran away from your husband—you don't feel like you need him?"

"What do you mean?"

"I mean, you don't need a man?"

"You mean, you want to sleep with me? You want me?"

"No!" Ajo Kawir said, taken aback. He hadn't anticipated that

Jelita would counterattack like that. "I have a wife. And I don't want to sleep with any other woman."

A small smile played at the corners of Jelita's lips.

—

She never wanted to see anyone. Only Gecko was allowed to come check in on her. Her parents had tried to come, but she didn't want to see them. Her in-laws were also forced to go home without a visit.

But all the same, that old man saw her. The warden and the guards were powerless to prevent him—even though she didn't want to see him, they still brought the old man into her cell, and now he was sitting right in front of her.

"I'm Uncle Bunny. I think your husband probably told you about me," he said.

Of course, Iteung thought.

"You don't need to worry about him. He's fine. Gecko probably already told you. After he got out of jail, he became a truck driver. He has his own truck and he travels around, covering all the roads in Java and Sumatra. He's just as strong as ever."

"He doesn't love me anymore," Iteung said. She turned away, trying to avoid Uncle Bunny's gaze.

"That's not true. As far as I know, he misses you terribly. You know what the problem is."

Iteung nodded, but still hid her face.

"There's one thing, though, that I'm sure Gecko never told you."

"What?"

"Gecko always brings him pictures of the little girl. Your daughter. Ajo Kawir himself asks for them. He sticks the pictures on the ceiling of his truck cabin, right over the wheel. He looks at them before he goes to sleep, and the moment he wakes up. He looks at her all along the journey. He takes good care of your child. He sends all his money back to her."

Now Iteung looked over at Uncle Bunny. Her eyes were wet.

———

Iteung lived in a cell with a middle-aged woman who had massacred seven men. Seven thieves broke into her house: her husband was murdered the night of the robbery, and her daughter was raped. After her daughter killed herself, that woman vowed she would get revenge. She tracked down those seven thieves and killed them one by one. Her life would end in prison—she'd been spared the death penalty, but she'd have to languish there for the rest of her days—and she was gracious enough to leave Uncle Bunny and Iteung alone in the cell.

"I've dealt with many things in my life, from war to servants who ran out on me. I've massacred communists. I've killed East Timorese freedom fighters. I've been pissed on by a dog. But nothing has ever burdened my thoughts like you two. I honestly and truly want to see you both happy."

"Thank you, Uncle."

"Maybe I only have one or two years left to live. I feel like such a fool for having wasted my life just screwing up the lives of others. At least, before I die, I want to solve your problems. I want to see you two happy, and more than that, I want the same for your children and your grandchildren."

"I want to be happy too, Uncle. But I don't know how anymore."

———

He came out of a convenience store with a plastic bag filled with snacks for the road, some cans of soda, and bath supplies. He walked toward the truck. The front door was ajar, and he saw the girl sitting inside the cabin, still reading her pulp novel. Her legs were crossed. He could see her bare thighs. Her thighs really weren't that enticing but, who knows why, for some reason the sight made him go hot and then cold.

"Don't tell me you want her," he whispered to the Bird, but it sounded like he was whispering to himself.

Ajo Kawir had no other choice but to continue to his truck, growing increasingly agitated.

—

No matter what, those wet dreams made him happy—at least he knew that the Bird could get up, and spew, even if only in his sleep. Before sleeping, sometimes the only thing he wished for was a wet dream, not caring that once he woke up, because he'd have to go wash himself off.

Sometimes, he even tried to direct these dreams himself. A few times he'd been able to control how the dream went but other times, the dream went its own way. Still, the main characters were always the same: him and Jelita. He was never able to substitute any other woman in her place, no matter how hard he tried.

—

"How long has it been since you slept with a woman?" Jelita asked, looking over at Ajo Kawir.

"A long time."

"You don't want it? You don't want to try it?"

Damn, though Ajo Kawir. This woman is out of control aggressive. Sooner or later, my defense will crack. "No. I don't want it."

—

When Ajo Kawir went into the bathroom at the next gas station, before he could close the door Jelita pushed her way in. He didn't know how she could be in the men's bathroom, but clearly she was now in there with him. With extraordinary composure, Jelita closed the door and locked it.

He couldn't believe this was happening but it was: looking at each other in that small space, Jelita smiled faintly, while Ajo Kawir could tell he was deathly pale.

Then the woman approached him, touched his cheek. Jelita stood on her tiptoes, kissed his lips. Ajo Kawir didn't move, wondering whether all of this was a dream, or actually happening, but he didn't have time to ask any questions. Jelita hugged him, and then she kissed him.

Finally Jelita got down on her knees and began to undo the fly of Ajo Kawir's jeans. When his pants hung down around his knees, even Ajo Kawir was mesmerized. He saw his bird stand up. Erect, big, pointing up to the sky. He had never seen the Bird looking so beautiful.

—

Coming out of the bathroom, Ajo Kawir was still wondering whether it had been a dream. Of course it hadn't, he thought. Even the stupidest person in the world can tell the difference between a dream and real life.

He had never made love before—in all honesty, that was the first time he'd had sex. He had never known how good it felt, even in a cramped bathroom. Sometimes Jelita had stood leaning against the wall, and he had pressed against her. Other times Jelita had sat on the edge of the water trough and Ajo Kawir had stood facing her, while her two legs wrapped around his body.

They didn't need a marital bed, they didn't need a hotel room, they didn't need a bamboo mat unfurled on white sand for incredible lovemaking. Even a tiny bathroom in a gas station would do. Ajo Kawir knew that now. He was happy. He felt a bit awkward, but he was also happy.

He looked all around for Jelita. The woman had left the bathroom first, and now he wanted to see her.

—

Ajo Kawir walked toward his parked truck, opened the cabin door, and didn't find her there.

"Jelita?" he almost yelled, calling out for her.

There was no answer. His eyes swept the entire gas station, past the attendant and people passing by, searching for Jelita's figure. He didn't see her. Ajo Kawir began to grow uneasy. He went back to the bathrooms, walking into the women's room, and standing there a moment.

"Jelita!?" Now he was screaming. But still there was no reply.

"Have you seen the woman who was with me?" Ajo Kawir asked the gas station attendant. He was sure that the attendant would have recognized Jelita, because she had been sitting next to him when he'd gotten gas, before they parked.

"No I haven't, I just saw her before, when she was with you."

Ajo Kawir was now in a panic. He rushed out of the gas station, approaching a food stall and a convenience store not far away. But there was no sign of Jelita. He ran back to the truck, and Jelita's small suitcase was gone. In fact, not one of the woman's things was there.

He waited at the gas station until nightfall. He spent the night in the nearest town and returned to the pump the following morning. He waited there the whole day.

Jelita did not appear again.

—

Iteung was lying down and studying two photographs—photographs of the two policemen. Uncle Bunny had given them to her.

"There's only one way to regain your happiness. I found them and I already told your husband, but prison and that damned bird changed his life so much. It's a real pity. He doesn't want to kill those two policemen. He doesn't want to kill anyone. He doesn't even want to fight with anyone."

"Why don't *you* kill them?"

"It's true I could have them killed, the country won't miss two jerk policemen. I'd never do it myself, I'd send someone to bump them off. But what's the point? Your husband is the one who should be holding a grudge. Only Ajo Kawir should kill them, so that his bird can get up again."

"Are you *sure* his pecker will be able to get up again?"

"I'm positive. Or at least, even if his bird doesn't get up again, he will have gotten his revenge. And I can die in peace."

"So what should I do, Uncle?"

"Convince your husband to do it. Convince him to kill those two policemen, get his revenge."

"He's not going to want to do that. He has chosen a peaceful path."

—

This middle-aged woman who had killed seven men always seemed at peace. Apparently, she never regretted what she had done.

"These were things I had to do, things much more important to me than freedom. I chose to end my life here rather than live on the outside, free but suffering because I hadn't done what needed to be done."

Iteung felt that her suffering could not be compared to what this woman was suffering. She was always happy to see her happy.

"But in any case, this isn't the place for you. You have to continue to live your life out there. I'm glad that tomorrow you will be set free."

Iteung just smiled. She didn't know what was waiting for her on the outside. She didn't yet foresee happiness—the greater likelihood was that just another kind of misery awaited her.

—

"No one's coming to pick you up, Iteung?" the prison guard asked when he saw her getting ready.

"Nope," Iteung replied. "I didn't want anyone to come—I'm heading home by myself."

"Are you sure?"

"As sure as I am of the fact that one day we are all going to die."

"I hope you don't get put in here again."

—

Ajo Kawir held the photo out to the kid, saying, "You forgot this."

The kid took it, and examined it. He smiled.

"How are you getting home?"

"An older soldier called me an ambulance. They're going to take me back to my village."

"I'm happy that you finally get to see your sweetheart again. What was her name? Nina? Yeah, Nina. With your money, you two can run away and start a new life together."

"Well, actually, she's not really my sweetheart."

"Oh no?" Ajo Kawir was a little surprised. He always thought she was the kid's girlfriend but maybe the girl's parents didn't approve of the relationship or something like that. He quickly realized that had just been the kid's fantasy.

"She's a whore. A whore who laughed at me."

"Why did she laugh at you?"

"I'm a one-pump chump. She barely touched it and I blew my load."

—

The kid was sitting in the ambulance, his two legs stretched out in front of him. There was no other way to send him home except in an ambulance. The cast on his leg wouldn't come off for months.

"The soldiers are being so good to me," the kid said.

"Of course they are, Dummy. They made a lot of money off of your fight."

Gaptooth Mono laughed. He held out a marker, and asked Ajo Kawir to write something on his cast. Ajo Kawir signed his name there.

"And where are you going after this, big brother?"

"I'm going to see my little daughter. I'm going to stop driving this truck. I'm tired, I'm going to let someone else drive it. If there's any money left over, I'm going to buy a new truck and look for another driver. Now tell me, what are you going to do with your money?"

"I'm going to pay Nina. I'm going to sleep with her every night for weeks straight, until my money is spent, until I collapse."

"Foolish kid."

—

She'd never forget that day. There was a knock on the front door, and when she opened it, she saw Iteung carrying a little red-faced infant. Iteung handed the baby over. For a few moments daughter-in-law and mother-in-law looked at each other.

"Mother, take care of this child."

"Iteung, what are you going to do? Where are you going?"

"I'm going to look for my husband, Mother."

"I don't know what happened with you two. I don't know where that son of mine went. As soon as you find him, please both of you return."

"Thank you, Mother."

Holding back tears, Iteung kissed the little baby girl and left.

—

Good Budi was guarding an empty house that belonged to an ex-government official. It was boring work—most work is, in fact, quite boring—until he found her inside the house, without knowing how she got in there.

"Iteung, my darling! How are you?"

"I'm great."

"You've been gone for so long. I heard you were pregnant. Whose child is it? Is it mine, or does it belong to that shithead beggar?"

"It's not yours."

—

Iteung knew right away that Good Budi had gone soft. It wasn't hard for her to beat him up, make his nose leak, split his lip, and crush his fingers.

Good Budi shrieked, "Iteung, what are you doing?"

Iteung did not deign to reply. She threw punches at Good

Budi's chin. She hurled him into a corner of the house. Iteung didn't want to give him any opportunity to run. She attacked him. She yanked a fistful of Good Budi's hair, grabbed it, and then slammed his head against the wall with all her might. She was sure his skull cracked.

Good Budi stopped shrieking. His body collapsed on the ground and didn't move. Blood flowed across the floor.

—

The policeman at the security post was shocked to see a woman, her hands covered in blood, walking toward him. Now she was standing right in front of him.

"Mr. Policeman, I killed someone."

The policeman stood frozen. The woman held out her wrists, asking to be handcuffed. The cop fumbled around nervously for a while, looking for his cuffs. After finding them, he finally shackled Iteung's wrists.

"Who did you kill?"

"His name is Good Budi."

"One of the Empty Hand?"

—

"How does it feel to be out of prison, Iteung?" asked the guard escorting her out through the gate.

"Amazing. I don't regret killing Good Budi. I don't regret it, even though I had to spend years in this cell."

"If you ask me, you did the right thing."

—

He felt strange having to drive the truck all by himself. He had driven it alone before, but many things made him feel strange this time. First, his truck was empty, he wasn't hauling anything at all, and he didn't feel upset by that. Second, he was taking a route he had never taken before, to the little town where it had all begun. My wife will soon be out of jail, he thought, do I really want to see her? Do I really want to see my little girl? Do I really dare go home? The questions swirled in his head, like a pile of dry leaves blown about, scattered by a truck wheel.

—

Driving along a deserted road, with dense teak forests to his left and right, Ajo Kawir stopped his truck, took a bottle of water and gulped it down, swallowing audibly. He was silent and still for a while, watching the occasional vehicle drive past. Then he looked down, pulled down his fly, and took out his dick.

"Bird," he said, "I don't know whether you'll ever get up again or not. I don't care. But I'm going home. I'm going to see my wife. She's getting out of jail today. Iteung and I are going to raise that little girl together."

—

Many things had happened in his life, but he didn't know what was behind all of it. He often wondered, why did Uncle Bunny send people to a Krakatoa crater and why did he want the Tiger dead? Why did Agus Cornpipe have to die, and why did Scarlet Blush have to go crazy? Why did there have to be any crazy women at all? Was there something behind all of this, something that made his bird refuse to stand up? He didn't know where all of this was going to end, just as he didn't know where any of it had really begun. He had gotten such scarce explanation for it all that he still didn't understand, not even a little bit. He might be able to ask Iwan Angsa, or Ki Jempes, or Uncle Bunny, but he finally decided not to.

"The more you know, the more problems you have," Gecko had once said.

And one problem—the Bird—had already been enough to destroy his life. He didn't need any more.

—

He was calmly driving the truck, slowly. Then suddenly he slammed on the brakes and pulled over to the shoulder, as if something had happened. He pulled down his pants again, took out his dick.

"Bird," he said, "Do you realize something?"

The hum of the idling engine was carried by the wind.

"That ugly woman, Jelita. Don't you feel like you recognized her?"

High in the treetops, the leaves rustled against one another.

"She was ugly. Super ugly. But when you looked at her, didn't you feel like you'd seen her before? I think she reminded me of that woman."

The sound of rushing water came from somewhere, maybe a nearby brook.

"That crazy woman. Scarlet Blush. I don't know why, but I think they're the same woman."

—

Scarface would never have guessed that his death would come so quickly. The woman was upon him. He didn't know her, but she knew about his past, knew about the night he had forced himself on a crazy woman. He didn't know what this woman had to do with the crazy woman, and she didn't explain.

"I just have to kill you, for the sake of my husband's private parts."

"What do you mean?"

"He should be the one coming here to get his revenge. But I assure you, he wouldn't deign to dirty his hands with your blood, so I am getting his revenge for him."

It didn't take Iteung very long to send the man to hell.

—

The Clove Smoker was found sprawled out in his kitchen, his neck broken. Dead, of course.

The gardener swore he saw a woman go in and he overheard her say:

"I just got out of prison for killing someone, and I don't mind going back for killing you."

—

Finally he saw his little girl. Her face reminded him of Iteung. With darkish skin, an oval face, shining eyes, and straight black hair. She looked just like she had in all the photos, which he'd stuck on the ceiling of his truck cabin, one after another.

The girl just stood there looking at him for a long time, her eyes asking, who are you?

"I'm your father," Ajo Kawir said.

The girl was surprised for a moment, but then she ran to hug him, and she wept. He heard, in a whisper, the little girl calling him Daddy. He returned her embrace, stroked her hair. Then the girl looked up and asked:

"Daddy, where's Mama? Grandma said Mama would come home today." The girl spoke without moving from Ajo Kawir's lap.

Her grandfather, the public library employee, and her grandmother smiled.

"She'll surely come. Maybe she's still on her way."

"Is that what she told you yesterday?"

"Maybe she had to take care of some business first. Daddy's sure, today she will come."

Then they heard a knock on the door.

—

They both sat on the bed, facing each other, cross-legged. Iteung wept. Ajo Kawir took her hand.

"You came back," Iteung said.

"Yes, I came back."

"I don't care whether you forgive me or not, I want to be with you. I love you."

"I love you too, Iteung. I'm going to stay here and live with you. We can take care of the child. She's beautiful, just like you."

Iteung laid her head in Ajo Kawir's lap.

They heard some commotion outside the bedroom.

"I think we have a visitor," Iteung said.

"Who?"

"The police."

"Mama, don't leave again!" the little girl whimpered. She grabbed Iteung's hand, trying to lead her back into the bedroom.

"Be patient, child. Now your daddy is here with you."

"Iteung, what happened?" asked Ajo Kawir.

"I killed those two policemen, my love. Those two old friends of yours."

"Dammit, Iteung!"

—

Ajo Kawir awoke in the morning and looked over to the empty space in the bed beside him. Iteung should be lying here, he thought. And then he realized something: he had an erection. He immediately sat up, pulled down his pants, and looked at the Bird, wonderstruck. As if he didn't believe it, he took it in his hand, stroked it. The Bird wriggled, got bigger and harder.

"Bird, you woke up! You really truly woke up!"

"Yes, Master. I'm so happy to be awake and feel so full of life."

"You fool! I can't give you anything. My wife is gone and I don't know how long she'll be in jail this time. She killed two police officers."

"I will wait for her patiently, just like you patiently waited for me to wake up, Master, all these years. But for the time being, while I'm waiting, may I go back to sleep?"

2011–2014

'A literary child of Gabriel García Márquez,
and Salman Rushdie' *New York Review of Books*

Eka Kurniawan

BEAUTY IS A WOUND

'An unforgettable, all-encompassing epic' *Publishers Weekly*

PUSHKIN
PRESS

PUSHKIN PRESS

Pushkin Press was founded in 1997, and publishes novels, essays, memoirs, children's books—everything from timeless classics to the urgent and contemporary.

Our books represent exciting, high-quality writing from around the world: we publish some of the twentieth century's most widely acclaimed, brilliant authors such as Stefan Zweig, Marcel Aymé, Teffi, Antal Szerb, Gaito Gazdanov and Yasushi Inoue, as well as compelling and award-winning contemporary writers, including Andrés Neuman, Edith Pearlman, Eka Kurniawan, Ayelet Gundar-Goshen and Chigozie Obioma.

Pushkin Press publishes the world's best stories, to be read and read again. To discover more, visit www.pushkinpress.com.

═══

THE SPECTRE OF ALEXANDER WOLF
GAITO GAZDANOV

'A mesmerising work of literature' Antony Beevor

SUMMER BEFORE THE DARK
VOLKER WEIDERMANN

'For such a slim book to convey with such poignancy the extinction of a generation of "Great Europeans" is a triumph' *Sunday Telegraph*

MESSAGES FROM A LOST WORLD
STEFAN ZWEIG

'At a time of monetary crisis and political disorder… Zweig's celebration of the brotherhood of peoples reminds us that there is another way' *The Nation*

THE EVENINGS
GERARD REVE

'Not only a masterpiece but a cornerstone manqué of modern European literature' Tim Parks, *Guardian*

BINOCULAR VISION

EDITH PEARLMAN

'A genius of the short story' Mark Lawson, *Guardian*

IN THE BEGINNING WAS THE SEA

TOMÁS GONZÁLEZ

'Smoothly intriguing narrative, with its touches of sinister,
Patricia Highsmith-like menace' *Irish Times*

BEWARE OF PITY

STEFAN ZWEIG

'Zweig's fictional masterpiece' *Guardian*

THE ENCOUNTER

PETRU POPESCU

'A book that suggests new ways of looking at the world
and our place within it' *Sunday Telegraph*

WAKE UP, SIR!

JONATHAN AMES

'The novel is extremely funny but it is also sad and
poignant, and almost incredibly clever' *Guardian*

THE WORLD OF YESTERDAY

STEFAN ZWEIG

'*The World of Yesterday* is one of the greatest memoirs of the twentieth
century, as perfect in its evocation of the world Zweig loved, as it is
in its portrayal of how that world was destroyed' David Hare

WAKING LIONS

AYELET GUNDAR-GOSHEN

'A literary thriller that is used as a vehicle to explore big
moral issues. I loved everything about it' *Daily Mail*

FOR A LITTLE WHILE

RICK BASS

'Bass is, hands down, a master of the short form, creating in a few pages
a natural world of mythic proportions' *New York Times Book Review*

JOURNEY BY MOONLIGHT
ANTAL SZERB

'Just divine… makes you imagine the author has had private access to your own soul' Nicholas Lezard, *Guardian*

BEFORE THE FEAST
SAŠA STANIŠIĆ

'Exceptional… cleverly done, and so mesmerising from the off… thought-provoking and energetic' *Big Issue*

A SIMPLE STORY
LEILA GUERRIERO

'An epic of noble proportions… [Guerriero] is a mistress of the telling phrase or the revealing detail' *Spectator*

FORTUNES OF FRANCE
ROBERT MERLE

1 *The Brethren*

2 *City of Wisdom and Blood*

3 *Heretic Dawn*

'Swashbuckling historical fiction' *Guardian*

TRAVELLER OF THE CENTURY
ANDRÉS NEUMAN

'A beautiful, accomplished novel: as ambitious as it is generous, as moving as it is smart' Juan Gabriel Vásquez, *Guardian*

A WORLD GONE MAD
ASTRID LINDGREN

'A remarkable portrait of domestic life in a country maintaining a fragile peace while war raged all around' *New Statesman*

MIRROR, SHOULDER, SIGNAL
DORTHE NORS

'Dorthe Nors is fantastic!' Junot Díaz

RED LOVE: THE STORY OF AN EAST GERMAN FAMILY
MAXIM LEO

'Beautiful and supremely touching… an unbearably poignant description of a world that no longer exists' *Sunday Telegraph*